A King Production presents…

All I See Is The Money…

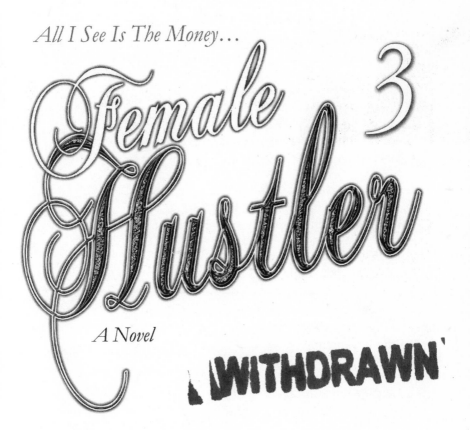

Female Hustler 3

A Novel

JOY DEJA KING

Cover concept by Joy Deja King
Cover model: Joy Deja King
Editor: Jacqueline Ruiz: tinx518@aol.com
Library of Congress Cataloging-in-Publication Data;

A King Production
Female Hustler Part 3/by Joy Deja King
For complete Library of Congress Copyright info visit;

www.joydejaking.com
Twitter: @joydejaking

A King Production
P.O. Box 912, Collierville, TN 38027

This Book is Dedicated To My:

Family, Readers, and Supporters.
I LOVE you guys so much. Please believe that!!

—Joy Deja King

"Good Girls Are Bad Girls
That Never Get Caught..."

A KING PRODUCTION

All I See Is The Money...

Female 3
Hustler

A Novel

JOY DEJA KING

Chapter One

Dangerous Woman

The private jet landed at the Kendall-Tamiami Executive Airport at seven in the morning, catching the brilliant and intense Miami sunrise. The fiery oranges and reds that illuminated the sky gave the perfect foreshadowing of what was to come. When the door opened, three armed guards dressed in all black appeared first before Angel stepped off the flight. Her hair was slicked back in a ballerina bun with oversized gold-plated sunglasses and a loose fitting button-down that resembled a man's dress shirt paired with distressed skinny jeans. She then softened the look by opting for ultra sexy slim heels and a red lippie with an oversized white clutch bag. The only jewelry worn was the massive diamond ring she was given on her wedding day. The look was a perfect balance of both masculine and feminine, which described Angel Blaze, who had now become a very dangerous woman.

"Wait!" She motioned to another armed guard who was behind her still on the jet. "Don't bring Darien out until the passenger door is open," she directed, waiting for the car to pull up.

It was no coincidence Angel chose to arrive at that particular airport and so early in the morning. She wanted them to arrive like a quiet storm so there would be no warning of their arrival. The couple had stayed in Hawaii where they were married and Darien was shot on their wedding day. For the last several weeks, Angel wanted to give her husband as much time to recuperate and regain his strength as needed. It had reached a point where the doctors had done all they could and Angel believed Darien would only be able to get better being back in Miami with his own private doctors. It would be a long road to recovery for boxing champion Darien Blaze to ever reach his former glory again.

"Are you okay?" Angel asked her husband after he was seated in the car comfortably. She held his hand lovingly as the driver pulled off.

"Yeah, I'm good, how 'bout you, my love?" he replied, trying to sound much stronger than he appeared. At times it nearly broke Angel's heart to look at her husband. Due to his extreme weight loss from being in a coma and in the hospital for an extended period of time, he appeared to be almost fragile-like to her. Slowly he was beginning to regain his appetite, but again it was a process that took time. But Darien was her husband, the first man she had given her body to and she was committed to him wholeheartedly.

"My husband is by my side, so I have every-thing I need and want." Angel lifted his hand and kissed it.

"I know I haven't been able to give you everything you need, but..."

"Stop it," she said cutting him off. Angel knew Darien was referring to sex. They weren't able to have any since he was shot. It bothered Darien much more than Angel. It made him feel like less of a man and she hated that.

"A man is supposed to be able to make love to his wife."

"That will come. We've made love so many times before. I have more than enough memories to hold me over." She smiled, wanting to make him feel better.

"I know what you're trying to do, but it isn't working. I'm not able to be a real husband to you and there ain't no one to blame but that motherfuckin' Nico Carter."

"Calm down. You don't need to get yourself upset. Baby, we're good," Angel assured him. "And you are a real husband to me. Don't ever doubt that. You also don't need to worry about Nico Carter. I promise, he will pay with his life for what he's done to you... to us."

Angel turned and stared out the window. She didn't want Darien to see the pain in her eyes because she knew he would blame himself. But none of this was his fault. Her husband was right, there was only one person that needed to be held accountable for the agony in their lives and his name was Nico Carter. Angel wouldn't stop until he was dead.

Nico sat at his office desk staring at Angel's wedding pictures. Sadness swept through him because he wasn't able to be a part of his daughter's wedding. He thought about how beautiful she had looked and how with each passing day he continued to miss out on being a part of her life.

"So let me understand something, Nathan. You go all the way to Hawaii. My private investigator was able to get me these fuckin' pictures, but yet you couldn't figure out a way to get Angel and bring her to me?" Nico frowned, tossing the pictures down on his desk.

"It wasn't that simple." Nathan sighed.

"Well, what was so fuckin' complicated?"

"It was only a handful of people at the wedding, but the security was heavy. You stressed that you wanted her brought to you alive and unscathed. But a lot of blood would've been shed to get to her and there was no guarantee that some of it wouldn't have been hers."

"I see." Nico stood up and walked around from behind his desk. He folded his arms and put his head down as if in deep thought. "Angel's safety always comes first, but I need you to find her and bring her to me. Do you know where she is now?"

"I'm not sure. From my understanding they were going back to Las Vegas after the wedding in Hawaii," Nathan responded.

"I don't need your understanding, I need facts. Find out where she is," Nico ordered.

"Will do, but can I ask you a question?"

"What is it?" Nico asked.

"Why is it so important to you that I find Angel and bring her back alive?"

"Because I said so. You can go now... you're dismissed," Nico stated, not bothering to make eye contact with Nathan.

Nathan walked out without saying a word. Although he knew exactly why his boss wanted Angel alive, he wanted to see if Nico would admit it to him. *That nigga wanna keep it to himself that Angel is his daughter. I guess he see me as nothing more than a worker. Even with Elijah out the way, he wanna play me like a lower level employee. That's cool though 'cause I got something for you and your daughter Mr. Nico Carter*, Nathan thought to himself as he laughed out loud.

Chapter Two

Truth And Lies Intertwined

Knock... knock... knock...

Aspen continued to bang on Taren's door with no answer. She finally gave up and headed down the stairs back to her car. When she was about to drive off, she glanced in her rearview mirror and noticed a cab pulling up. A few seconds later, the taxi driver got out and popped the trunk to take out a suitcase. Then Taren opened the back door. She stepped out wearing a crop top with an elastic off-shoulder neckline, ruffled short sleeves with lemon tree print throughout, and paired it with denim shorts. She seemed relaxed and carefree. Aspen waited until the taxi drove off before she got out her car and ran up on Taren.

"Taren, where have you been!?" Aspen shouted.

Taren was startled and almost tripped backwards down the stairs when she turned around to see who was yelling. "Aspen, what the fuck! You scared me," Taren snapped, dropping her suitcase on the stairs. "Why the hell is you screaming my name?"

"I wanted to get your attention."

"Okay, well you have it now. What's up?"

"Why haven't you been returning my phone calls and text messages?" Aspen wanted to know. "You've been MIA for weeks."

"Angel gave us some time off so I decided to do some traveling. Is that all right wit' you," Taren said sarcastically, rolling her eyes as she continued to walk up the stairs towards her apartment. Aspen remained on her trail, following close behind her.

"I told you I needed to speak to you about Laurie." On the sly, Taren tried to shut the door on Aspen, but she wasn't having it and pushed it open before it could close. "Are you trying to ignore me?" Aspen asked, refusing to back down.

"Ain't nobody trying to ignore you," Taren said, sounding defensive. "I have shit to do, that's all."

"Oh, when you ready to party or looking for a weed hookup, you quick to return my call and text messages. But if I wanna ask you about our friend you get ghost. What sort of shit is that?" Aspen pressed.

"Fine!" Taren huffed, tossing her suitcase in her bedroom before storming back out into the living room where Aspen was standing. "What do you need to talk to me about regarding Laurie?"

"After we left the lounge did you see Laurie again that night?" Aspen's question was so blunt and direct it made Taren uncomfortable.

"No. I already told you I didn't see Laurie after that. Last time I saw Laurie was when we were all together at the lounge."

"That's the story you're sticking to?"

"Excuse me? What the fuck is that supposed to mean?"

"It means that if you didn't see Laurie before

she got killed how did her emerald earring end up in your apartment?" Aspen questioned with an accusatory finger pointing in Taren's direction.

"Emerald earring... girl, what is you talkin' about? I don't have no earring of Laurie's."

"I saw the earring in your apartment. I stepped on it and thought I broke it. I even commented on how pretty it was before you snatched it from me. Now do you remember the emerald earring I'm talking about?" Aspen's tone was ice cold. She was purposely being harsh with her delivery.

"Oh, that earring," Taren said casually. "I know exactly what you're talking about. That didn't belong to Laurie, it's mine."

"Okay, then go get *both* earrings." Aspen sneered with darts in her eyes, stressing the word both.

"No problem. I'll be right back." Taren could feel Aspen burning a hole in her back as she walked into her bedroom. She rummaged through her jewelry box loudly to make it seem like she was actually looking for the earrings when Taren knew damn well she didn't have them. She had actually tossed the one earring Aspen had stepped on in the trash weeks ago, wanting to get rid of all evidence that could link her to Laurie's murder.

"What's taking you so long, Taren? Hurry up!" Aspen yelled becoming impatient.

"I don't know what happened to those earrings." Taren threw up her hands. "I looked everywhere. I must've misplaced them."

"That's fine. Maybe the police will have better luck finding them." Aspen smiled as she walked towards the front door.

"Wait!" Taren screamed frantically. She reached out and grabbed Aspen's arm.

"Let go of me!" Aspen barked, snatching her arm away from Taren. "I ain't Laurie. I'll drag yo' ass all through this apartment and think nothing of it."

"No need for threats," Taren tried to reason. She needed to quickly figure out a different approach upon realizing that Aspen would be a tough cookie to crumble. "You're right."

"Right about what?" Aspen waited to see how Taren would respond.

"I did see Laurie again after the lounge. She came over here to talk to me."

"Talk to you about what?"

"About that guy Tony she saw me talking to at the lounge. I did know him and I told her the truth about it."

"What! How did you know him?"

"It's a long story, but I came clean with Angel about it. Tony was a client of Angel's Girls and I started seeing him on the side to make additional money so I could help out my drug-addicted mother. I was too embarrassed to tell anyone. When Laurie came over she was upset and I felt guilty that I let her leave like that, especially after she ended up dead."

"So you told Angel all of this?"

"Everything except for me seeing Laurie that night after we left the lounge. Like I said, I felt guilty that I let her leave here so upset. Maybe if I had made her stay here with me, she would still be alive." Taren let a few crocodile tears drop for good measure.

"I guess Laurie's earring must've dropped when she came over to talk to you," Aspen said as if believing Taren's story.

"Exactly. I'm actually relieved you confronted me about that night. I had been feeling so guilty, but it feels good to finally talk about it. It's like a burden has been lifted off of me."

"I'm glad you came clean with me. There's no sense in us having a falling out over a miscommunication. Well, let me go. I got a text earlier that I'm back on the clock tonight. I need to go home and get dressed."

"Okay. Let's hang out soon." Taren smiled.

"Of course. Talk to you later," Aspen said before leaving. "That lying bitch!" she mumbled after closing the door behind her. Aspen cursed Taren out the entire time she walked to her car. Once inside, she gripped the steering wheel and looked up. She could see Taren peeking through the blinders watching her.

"I don't know what the fuck you're hiding Taren, but that bullshit story you just told me was to get me off your back, but it ain't working," Aspen said, talking out loud as she drove off. "But I see what type of hoe yo' ass is, so I gotta play this carefully. Plus, Angel is your bestie, so I can't bring nothing to her without some certifiable receipts. I need my job and I'm not trying to get fired because she take your side over mine. I have no evidence to take to the police beside that emerald earring I'm sure your trifling ass already tossed. No worries though, 'cause tricks like you always fuck up. You on my radar now, so when you make that wrong move, I'll be right there to get what I need to bring yo' ass all the way down. I will get justice for you, Laurie," Aspen promised herself.

Angel watched as Darien slept peacefully. She had already seen a change in his mood since leaving Hawaii and being in their new home. Darien had bought the house as a surprise wedding gift for her. He had it decorated and completely furnished. The day they arrived back in Miami was the very first time Angel even saw the house, but she was in love the moment they pulled into the winding driveway. The home was strategically built on a 38k square feet peninsula with 480 feet of waterfront on prestigious Mashta Island. There were unimpeded wide panoramic views of the ocean, Bill Braggs Park, Cape Florida Lighthouse, and Stiltsville. It was their own private oasis in paradise and a place Angel prayed would heal her husband from the inside out.

Before Angel would allow herself to enjoy the beautiful home her husband bought for her, she had other pressing matters to deal with and it started tonight.

"Sorry it took me so long to get here, but I was handling a situation with the security de-tail," Keaton explained, standing up when he saw

Angel walking down the circular stairway.

"All is forgiven if you're here to tell me that you've located Nico Carter and he's dead." Keaton swallowed hard and pressed his lips together tightly. "Based on how uncomfortable you look, I take that as a no."

"The last I heard Nico was in New York. He's been there for some time now."

"People can still get got in New York. Why is that of any relevance?" Angel questioned.

"He moves very discreetly while in New York. His family is there, so they have a lot of security. It's extremely hard to get to him."

"Then maybe you're going about this wrong. Maybe you need to make Nico come to you," Angel suggested.

"I'm not following you." Keaton raised an eyebrow confused by what Angel was saying.

"Let's take a page out of Nico's book. He had me kidnapped to get to Darien. How about we kidnap the one he cherishes most. Does he have a wife, son, or daughter?"

"Angel, I don't think we need to take that route."

"Why the fuck not?" she scoffed standing face to face with Keaton. "Have you seen my husband? He doesn't even look like the same man.

He doesn't even feel like the same man and it's killing him and God forbid he isn't able to fight again. It will destroy him. Nico Carter is the person responsible for doing this to my husband and he will pay! So if that means you kill his wife, son, or daughter then so be it."

"Angel, you don't know what you're doing. I have to tell..."

"What's going on out here?" Darien asked coming down the hallway. Angel and Keaton both looked up.

"Darien, what are you doing out of bed? You're supposed to be resting." Angel ran up the stairs before her husband could come down.

Keaton observed from a distance as Angel held onto Darien and took him back to their bedroom. He shook his head in frustration. He was on the verge of revealing all to Angel until Darien showed up. The two men had been friends for years. They were like brothers and his loyalty ran deep, but keeping this secret was a heavier burden than Keaton could deal with.

Angel is so fuckin' determined to take down Nico Carter by any means necessary without understanding the ramifications. She needs to know the truth before making a decision that she'll live to regret. Darien, you my nigga for life, but I can't let Angel do this. I have to put an end to this shit before it's too late, Keaton thought to himself, deciding he would be the one to tell Angel the truth.

Chapter Three

Sweet Design

Dominique was on stage shaking her ass like rent was due tomorrow. Technically it was due a week ago, but after begging and pleading, her landlord gave her until Monday morning to come up with her rent money. So while most were at church praying on a Sunday afternoon, Dominique was doing her own praying by working a double shift at the damn near empty strip club.

Unfortunately for Dominque, stage name Candi Girl, she was shaking that ass in the wrong city. She could shake, twerk, and do cartwheels on that stage and Dominique would be lucky to leave with one hundred dollars in her garter belt. Living in a small town right outside of Alabama, there were no NBA players, rappers, or big money spenders coming through the door. Instead, she dealt with blue collar workers who thought they were doing her a favor by slipping her a twenty.

Dominique was beginning to think that at the ripe old age of twenty-one, it was time for her to retire. But somebody must've been listening to all that praying Candi Girl was doing on stage because today her luck had changed when Desmond aka The Black Knight walked through the doors.

"Excuse me, can you get me and my friend here a couple of beers," the guy said to Dominique.

"I'm not a waitress, but I'll get somebody for you," she told him.

"You not a waitress, what you do? Dance?"

"Didn't you just see me come off the stage? So yes, I dance," Dominique snapped.

"My fault, shorty. No need to get hostile. I just walked in. I'm Miles. Why don't you sit down and have a drink with me."

"No thanks. I have to be back on stage in a few minutes. I'll go get a waitress for you," Dominique said rushing off.

"Why you fuckin' wit' that girl?" Desmond shook his head.

"I ain't fuckin' wit' her. I'm tryna get wit' her. That bitch bad. I damn sure wasn't expecting to see nothing like that working in this hole in the wall."

"When this nigga gon' be here?" Desmond asked. "'Cause this place right here some garbage. He couldn't come up with a better place for us to meet?" Desmond looked around in disgust at the rundown club. "I'm ready to go."

"He said he was on the way. Let me call him again. I'm telling you, he the right dude to handle the product in this area. We can bring in a couple of our other workers to oversee this nigga and make sure he handling business right," Miles explained.

"Yo, you can stop tryna sell me on this shit. I'm here ain't I. I just wanna meet the nigga so we can go," Desmond huffed, regretting he had agreed to show up until Dominique took the stage. Even with the poor lighting, raggedy stage, and subpar dancing attire, Dominique was able to shine. She resembled a modern day, rough around the edges version of Dorothy Dandridge. But those rough edges gave Dominique the skills to seduce the stage like she was working at a high end establishment in Vegas instead of slumming it.

"I told you that bitch was bad," Miles commented, noticing Desmond engrossed in her performance. "I don't understand why a chick that look like that working up in here. She need to be dancing in one of yo' clubs."

"Me neither and you right." Desmond remained immersed in Dominique's dance moves until her set was done and she came off the stage. "Excuse me, Miss," he waved his hand calling her over. He could see that she was hesitating for a minute so he pulled out a hundred dollar bill letting her know this was business.

"Listen, all I do is dance. I ain't fuckin' you," Dominique stated, eyeing the one hundred dollar bill Desmond was holding.

"You don't even have to dance for me. All I want to do is talk."

"You wanna pay me a hundred dollars to talk?"

"A hundred dollars was just for you to come over here. I'll give you another four hundred to talk." Desmond laid the money on the table so Dominique would know the offer was real.

Dominique didn't even try to contain her excitement, but before she got too happy she asked, "This money ain't counterfeit is it?"

"Nah." Desmond laughed. "I wouldn't do you like that."

"Good, 'cause I need this money to pay my rent. Thank you so so much!" Dominique exclaimed sitting down.

Desmond smiled. He dealt with all sorts of women in his line of business. Some worked for him moving drugs, in his clubs; others he dated. All of them were from different walks of life, but had one thing in common; they thought they were hot shit. With the money women had made working for him or he'd given women he'd dated, none had ever said thank you. Instead, they wanted more money for shoes, clothes, jewelry, cars, and material things. Never did he hear them say they needed money to pay their rent. Hearing Dominique's honesty was a breath of fresh air for a man living in such a convoluted world.

"Tell me. Why is a girl as pretty as you working in this shit hole?"

"I guess you don't sugar coat nothing." Dominique giggled. "This place is pretty shitty, but there's not that many options for somebody who doesn't even have their high school diploma.

I only have my GED."

"I feel you on that, but you ain't gonna make no money working at a strip club like this. This money I gave you is probably more than you make in a week."

"A week! Shit make that a month. Luckily my rent is only two hundred and fifty dollars."

"Where you learn to dance like that?" Desmond nodded towards the stage. "You move like you're a professional dancer and you built like one too," he said, noticing how toned her body was.

"I've always loved to dance since I was a little girl. I can watch a dance routine on television and learn the choreography just like that." She snapped her finger. "Before she died, my mother used to tell me I was her little star. She even named me after the character Dominique Deveraux from Dynasty. My mother would boast and say that was the first Black Bitch on TV and she owned that character. She loved her some Diahann Carroll." Dominique laughed. "So when I'm up on that stage, I always put on a performance like there are a room full of people watching me."

"So why are you working here? There's other strip clubs where a room full of people would be watching you and you can make some real paper."

"I hear you. I wanted to work at a club in Atlanta or something, but it cost money to move. I'm barely surviving here. Having you come in today and give me this five hundred dollars for a conversation is the best thing that has happened to me in years."

"You don't have any family?"

"Both my mother and father died years ago. I have some family here, but they doing worse than me, if that's even possible."

"You ain't got no man?"

Dominique shook her head no. "Not any-more."

"What happened?" Desmond wanted to know.

"That nigga begged me to move to Charlotte with him. He got a good job at a bank. He said he was gonna pay for me to go back to school. When I moved there, all he wanted to do was keep me locked in the house. Then I found out he was screwing some chick that worked with him at the bank, so I packed my shit and came back home. Now I'm here, broke as hell, but at least I'm not dealing wit' no cheatin' ass nigga."

"I wanna help you out," Desmond announced.

"Why?" Dominique's face was full of confusion and shock.

"A lot of people call me The Black Knight. I like helping people, but that ain't really the reason they call me that. I'm talking in circles right now," he joked.

"Yeah, you are," she agreed.

"Look, I think you are gorgeous. Not only that, but you really do have skills up there. Yeah, you need to polish up your look, but you can be a beast on the pole and make a ton of money."

"So how can you help me? Do you know somebody that has a legit club I can work at and make money?"

"Yep, my club."

"You own a strip club?"

"Yes. One of the top strip clubs in Miami."

"I knew you weren't from around here!" Dominique's face lit up. "The way you dress, talk, and all that money. Wow! Miami! Are you saying I can come work at your club in Miami?"

"Yes, that's what I'm saying."

"But where will I live; how will I get there?"

"I got you covered on all your expenses. Trust me, if you put on a performance like you just did on that stage, you'll be able to pay me back after your first night working. I guarantee it. You're gonna make my club a lot of money and in return you'll make yourself a ton of cash.

"I don't even know your name besides the Black Knight," Dominique said.

"I'm Desmond."

"Desmond, you not bullshittin' me, is you? 'Cause I'm ready to pack up the one suitcase I got and leave tonight." Desmond started laughing. "Why you laughing at me? Is this all a joke?"

"No... no... no. Nothing like that. You just funny to me in a cute way. I love how excited you are. People I deal wit', don't nothing excite them no more. They done did it all. You, you different, but once you get in this life, you'll change too. So for now, I'm enjoying the Dominque of today."

"Listen, I ain't neva gonna change. I'ma still be the same girl I am right now."

"Hmmm. I know you believe that, but I've seen it time and time again. Once you get introduced to this life, you'll never be the same again. So get ready."

"Man, if it will get me out of this going nowhere town, then show me the way." Dominque shrugged.

"Then go home and pack your bags," Desmond stated.

"Miami here I come!" Dominique jumped up and cheered.

Chapter Four

Sorry Not Sorry

"Good morning, ladies!" Angel looked out at all the women sitting down in front of her.

"Good morning!" Angel's Girls said back. Each with a wide smile on their face.

"We're all so happy that you're back." Amber beamed. "And congrats on the wedding."

"Thanks so much." The girls heard that Angel had gone off to Hawaii and got married, but none of them knew what happened to Darien while they were there. Angel went out her way to keep it hush-hush, but now that she was back home, it would be almost impossible to keep it quiet.

"So give us all the details about the wedding. I know you looked beautiful," Aspen chimed in.

"Thank you. I will definitely share the details at a later time, but today I wanted to discuss Angel's Girls. I know I've been neglecting the business some. I have some personal issues I'm dealing with so I've decided to bring in a partner."

"A partner? What does that mean for us? Are other girls going to be brought in to replace us?" Monique wanted to know and so did all the other girls.

"No, nothing like that. You all are the heart of Angel's Girls. You will not be replaced, unless of course someone doesn't adhere to the rules. Other than that your job is safe."

"Will we be meeting this new partner?" Taren questioned.

"Yes, he will play an intricate role in running the business. It was important to me that I got a partner who would be involved in the day-to-day operation. He came highly recommended. He is the owner of several high-end strip clubs in and outside of Miami. We've spoken several times on the phone and through Skype. Now that we're both back in town we'll be having dinner tonight. He will be formally introduced to you all tomorrow," Angel informed them.

"So what's this mystery guy's name?" one of the other girls inquired.

"Desmond... Desmond Blackwell. He has a lot of connections with major ballers. That means more work for you ladies which means more money."

"We like that!" Aspen applauded.

"We all do!" The other ladies applauded too.

"I knew you would. We're taking Angel's Girls to the next level so get ready ladies. If you don't have any other questions then I'll see you tomorrow when you'll meet Mr. Blackwell."

"What do you think is going on with Angel... you know, in her personal life?" Monique whispered to Taren who was sitting next to her.

"I have no idea."

"Aren't you all best friends? I thought for sure you would know."

"Yes, we are best friends, but she did just get married," Taren snapped back. "So excuse me," Taren got up and left cringing inside. She did want to know what was going on with Angel. Clearly her anonymous tip to Nico didn't work as planned since Darien was still alive, but something went wrong and Taren was dying to know exactly what.

"It's so good to see you," Taren said giving Angel a hug. "I left you a couple messages, but I didn't want to be too intrusive. You are a married woman now," Taren teased.

"Yes, I am."

"So how was your honeymoon? Let's go have some drinks so you can give me all the details. I miss hanging out with my bestie."

"I miss you too, but I have a lot going on."

"Are you talking about those personal issues you mentioned?"

"Yeah." Taren could sense some sadness in Angel's tone.

"Well, tell me about it. You know you can talk to me about anything. That's what best friends are for."

"Thank you, Taren. I do need someone to talk, but not today. I need to get back home and check on Darien before I meet with my new partner. I'll call you soon though." Angel blew Taren a kiss and left out.

What in the hell is going on with you, Angel? You need to go home and check on Darien... that's a little odd. Did something happen to him and why are you being so secretive? So many questions and no answers. Then you have this new partner. You're such a control freak. For you to be bringing someone into your business means those personal issues you're having are pretty serious. I need to get to work and figure out what is going on, Taren thought to herself.

When Angel got home she rushed upstairs to check on her husband. Whenever Darien wasn't in her sight, she worried. Angel felt that he needed her more than ever so she wanted to be there for him at all times. When she got to their bedroom the door was slightly ajar and she could hear him arguing with someone. Angel's initial reaction was to barge in the room and tell whoever was making Darien upset to get the hell out, but she stopped herself when she heard whom he was arguing with. Instead of interrupting, she stopped and listened.

"We brothers! Your loyalty is to me," Darien barked.

"I have been loyal to you, but this I can't do. Angel deserves to know the truth and you need to tell her, 'cause I don't want no part of this," Keaton barked back.

"You are a part of this and you will keep your mouth shut. Angel can never know that Nico Carter is her father. Never!" Darien yelled.

"I'll keep my mouth shut and Nico will be killed. But you better pray your wife never learns the truth."

"I'll take care of my wife, you just make sure you take care of Nico."

"Nico is a done deal. There's no stopping that now, but this secret needs to stay between me and you."

Angel stood outside of the door barely able to hold herself up. She wanted to cry tears of joy, sadness, and anger. "Nico is my father... my father is alive," she mumbled under her breath. Angel wiped her tears away and pulled herself together before entering the bedroom. "Darien, is everything okay in here?" she asked as if nothing was wrong.

"Everything is fine, baby. Keaton and I were talking and things got a lil' heated."

"Oh, Keaton we never got to finish talking the other night. You were about to tell me some-thing. I'm available now if you want to finish our conversation," Angel said. Keaton and Darien eyed each other nervously.

"Keaton has some business he needs to handle for me. You all can finish your conversation later. Right, Keaton?" Keaton stared at Darien before glancing over at Angel.

"Is there something you want to say to me, Keaton?" Angel was giving him a chance to come clean, but he didn't take it.

"Darien's right. We can finish our conversation later."

"That's fine. You know your way out," Angel said coldly.

"I'll talk to you later, Darien." Angel followed Keaton out the bedroom and watched from the top of the stairs as he left without saying a word to him.

"Did Keaton leave?" Darien questioned when Angel came back into the bedroom.

"Yes, he's gone. It's just the two of us."

"Good. I like it that way. Come lay next to me," Darien told Angel. Instead, she sat at the end of the bed. "Why are you sitting so far away? Come closer. I've been waiting to hold you all day."

"I would come closer, but I'm afraid I might hurt you if I do," Angel stated coolly.

Darien gave Angel a curious stare. "Hurt me. Stop playin' and bring yo' fine ass over here."

Darien assumed his wife was having a little fun with him.

"You were going to let me kill my own father? What sort of fucked up individual are you?" Angel's voice was even and calm. So much so it sent chills up Darien's spine. "Why are you so damn quiet... did someone cut off your tongue?"

The color seemed to completely vanish from Darien's face. He struggled to speak or put a sentence together. "Baby, please let me explain," was the best he could come up with.

"Please do. Explain to me how you could know that the only family I had left in this world was alive, but not tell me. Explain how you could keep me from the one person, besides my mother, that I yearned to have a relationship with more than anything. Here's your chance to explain that to me."

"After Nico had you kidnapped and I didn't know if you were dead or alive, he caused havoc in our lives. When I found out the man who did that to us was your father, I didn't think he deserved to have you as a daughter."

"Oh, really. Well maybe I'm the one who doesn't deserve to have a father like Nico. It all makes sense now. Why he was trying so hard to keep me safe and went out his way to have me brought back after your men came and got me. He wanted to have a relationship with his daughter." A single tear escaped Angel's eye.

"Angel, I know you always felt like your life would've been different if you grew up with your father, but Nico Carter isn't right for you."

"You have some nerves. How dare you play God with my life! I had the right to decide whether I wanted a relationship with Nico, not you. Because you fucked up your business dealings with him, you took it upon yourself to shut him out of my life."

"It wasn't like that, Angel," Darien said wanting to plead his weak case.

"Was Nico even the person that shot you? Answer me, Darien!"

"Nico didn't actually pull the trigger, but I know he sent one of his men."

"How can you be so sure?"

"Because he's the only motherfucker that has it out for me and would have the means to track me down. It was Nico!" Darien was adamant.

"I don't believe it was him."

"What the fuck! Now that you know he's your father, all of sudden you don't believe he would have me killed?"

"Yes, that's what I'm saying. If he tracked

us down in Hawaii, he knew it was our wedding day. Nico clearly cares about me. He would never want to rip my heart out like that on my wedding day. Now that I know the truth, I don't believe that's the type of move he would make. It doesn't make sense. If anything he would try to stop the wedding, not kill you in the process after the fact."

"Angel, you're wrong. Nico is not this honorable man that you've made him out to be."

"You're in no position to talk about what an honorable man is. You better hope that I'm able to find Nico before anything happens to him. Because if my father's blood ends up on my hands because of you, I swear I won't rest until I ruin you."

"Baby, you don't mean that. You're hurt right now and I understand. I hate myself for causing you pain and I'm sorry. Don't let Nico Carter come between us."

"You!" Angel pointed her finger at Darien. "You came between us, not Nico. I can forgive you for almost anything but this!" From the distraught expression on Angel's face the pain ran deep. "You were the one person that knew how I had this empty void in my heart from not knowing either of my parents. At least with my mother, my grandmother always showed me pictures and I had things that belonged to her. But I knew absolutely NOTHING," Angel screamed, "about my dad. Not even his fuckin' name. I could be sitting down, getting to know him right now. But I'm here with you, the person responsible for keeping me away from my father."

"I'll make it up to you, I promise. You have to forgive me, Angel. I'm sorry. I'm so sorry, baby."

"No, you're not, but you will be," Angel made clear before storming out.

Chapter Five

Broken Glass

"You said you had some new information regarding Angel. What is it?" Nico asked Richard, the private investigator he had tracking Angel.

"The information isn't about Angel, but it does affect her directly. I think…"

"Just get to it, Richard," Nico scoffed, cutting him off.

Richard had worked with Nico for many years so he was used to his boss's abrasive delivery. "I already told you that Angel did get married while in Hawaii."

"Yep, unfortunately."

"I just found out that the reason I lost track of the bride and groom was because Darien Blaze was shot on their wedding night."

"What! Are you sure?" Nico put down the cognac he was about to pour himself and gave Richard his full attention.

"You know I wouldn't give you any half-ass information. I triple check my sources before I bring anything to you."

"True. That's why I've kept you employed for all these years. Tell me what else you know," Nico said taking off his suit jacket and getting comfortable on the couch.

"He was rushed to the hospital, but everything was kept under wraps. I can't even locate a police report. I do know that he was recuperating in Hawaii until recently, but I can't find any additional information after that."

"How serious were the injuries?"

"Life threatening, but they've gone through a lot of trouble for that information not to get out."

"That explains why Darien's upcoming fight was unexpectedly postponed." Nico rubbed his chin while nodding his head as if having an aha moment. "My thing is who shot him," he pondered.

"You're not going to want to hear this, but I believe I know."

A grimaced expression crept up on Nico's face. "Tell me," he said flatly.

"I think it's your guy Nathan. I did a little investigating because you know that's what I do." He smirked. "Nathan caught a flight out of Hawaii first thing the next morning after the shooting. If he was supposed to be looking for an opportunity to grab Angel, why would he leave so soon after the wedding. The only reason would be if Nathan knew it would be impossible to get her because she would be confined to a hospital not leaving her husband's side."

"But why would Nathan want to kill Darien?"

"Not sure, but I did some further digging and Nathan has been in touch with someone in Darien's camp frequently the last few months."

"That sneaky motherfucker. He's playing both sides, but what is his ultimate goal?" Nico huffed. "Whatever it is, it ain't good."

"I can keep digging. I'm sure there is a lot more information I can find on this Nathan character."

"Nah, you don't have to do that," Nico said.

"Are you sure?"

"Positive."

"Then what are you going to do?"

"Kill that sonofabitch! What you think," Nico sulked before standing up to go pour himself another drink.

"I know you're going to do what you want, but I think you should hold off on killing him."

"Now why in the fuck would I do that?" Nico questioned.

"I think you should let me follow him. See what else is going on. This could be just the tip of the iceberg. He might be planning something else or even working with someone else. Let me gather all the information I can that might be beneficial to you, then you can kill him."

"Make it quick 'cause I want that nigga dead. What you're saying does sound logical, but when you have a weak link in your circle, it has to be cut off immediately before that shit spread."

"I agree. I get why you want Nathan dead, but I feel there's more to this and I need him alive to find out what that is," Richard rationalized.

"I want you to check one other thing for me too."

"You name it."

"You know Elijah."

"Of course, he's worked for you for many years."

"Yes, and he's always been very loyal to me. Recently he got killed."

"Sorry to hear that, Nico. I know how much you value good workers."

"I do and Elijah was one of my best. Nathan was in Vegas with Elijah when he got killed. Supposedly, one of Darien's men shot him, but given what you've presented to me today, I'm questioning if that's what happened."

"You think Nathan is the one that shot and killed Elijah?" Richard questioned.

"Yes, and I need to know why."

"I'm on it."

"It's gonna take every ounce of my strength not to break that nigga's neck when he shows his face around here." Nico was becoming heated just thinking about it.

"I know, but it's imperative you don't let on that we are aware of what he's been up to. He's clearly very dangerous, so the less he knows the better. We can't raise any suspicion."

"Richard, I don't need a lecture. I know how to play this shit. I've dealt with deadlier devils than Nathan. That nigga better enjoy the time he got left on this Earth, 'cause it ain't much." Nico slammed down his glass, shattering it into a thousand pieces.

"Angel, I was surprised when you called and said you needed to talk. Is everything okay with Darien?" Keaton asked with concern.

"I guess you haven't spoken to him?"

"Not since earlier today when I saw him at the house. That's why I was surprised when I got your call since we had just seen each other."

"Earlier you mentioned that we never got to finish our conversation. I thought this was the perfect place for us to do that. You know... so we won't have any interruptions."

"Oh, that. It's nothing important."

"But it is important. So tell me Keaton, what burden are you carrying that's so heavy on your mind?"

"Like I said, it's not important. Is that why you called me? So I could come all this way for absolutely nothing." Keaton grumbled, irritated.

"I know that in the past you and Darien would meet here to discuss a lot of business. I figured this place was perfect for us to have that much needed conversation. Way out here in the middle of nowhere. No one to disturb us."

"Angel, no disrespect but can you get to the point. I have a lot of things I need to be handling for Darien, speaking of which," Keaton paused glancing down at his phone. "That's Darien calling now."

"Don't answer. Let it go to voicemail," Angel stated.

Keaton looked at Angel like she was crazy and proceeded to tap the accept button. "I don't know what's going on wit' you, but you buggin."

"Obviously you didn't hear what I said," Angel said gripping her gun in Keaton's direction. "Put down the phone."

"Yo, Angel what the fuck is wrong wit' you! You need to put that gun away."

"This is my last time telling you to put your phone down."

Keaton was debating on whether or not to do what Angel asked. He was more in shock than anything. Seeing her point a gun in his direction seemed out of character for her, but Keaton then wondered, maybe he didn't know Angel as well as he thought.

"You want me to put the phone down... I'll

put the phone down." Keaton placed his cell on the table beside him. He tried to maintain a cool demeanor not wanting shit to further escalate. "I put my phone down, do you think you can do the same and put away your gun?"

"No. What I can do is tell you why Darien was calling."

"Okay, I'm listening."

"He probably wanted to alert you that the secret you all share is no longer a secret."

"Not sure what secret you're referring to."

"Continue to play dumb, Keaton, but all you're doing is pissing me off more. You should've told me the truth about Nico."

"What about Nico?" Keaton wasn't sure if Angel was trying to run game on him or what, so he decided it was best to play it close to the chest. "Are you talking about what's taking so long for the hit to go down?"

"No, motherfucker. I'm talking about you letting me put a hit on my own father you sonofabitch." The hatred in Angel's eyes was brutal.

"Fuck," Keaton mumbled under his breath, lifting his hands behind his head in frustration. "I can't believe Darien decided to tell you the truth after he demanded I keep my mouth shut."

"Darien didn't tell me shit."

"Then how... oh damn," Keaton said putting the pieces together. "You must've overheard our conversation earlier today." He sighed, shaking his head. "Angel, I wanted to..."

"Save it!" she shouted, cutting Keaton off. "I gave you more than one opportunity to man the fuck up and do the right thing. But no, you decided to withhold the truth from me just like Darien did. The nerve of both of you."

"I get it. I tried to tell Darien he needed to be honest with you, but he was against it. I wanted you to know that Nico was your father, but it wasn't my place to tell you."

"The moment I told you I wanted Nico killed is when it became your place to tell me."

"Maybe you're right, but you have to understand. Darien is my brother. My loyalty is to him first."

"I get what you mean... family first. So you can understand why now you're on my shit list, right? Because Nico Carter is my family, so he comes first."

"Angel, you have every right to be upset. How can I make it right?"

"The first thing you're going to do is get on your phone and call off the hit," she ordered.

"I can't do that." Keaton sighed.

"What the fuck you mean, you can't do it?" Angel took a step forward, gripping the trigger even tighter.

"It's not that I don't want to, but I can't. Once the hit is placed there's no stopping it."

"What the hell do you mean there's no stopping it?! Pick up the phone, call the fuckin' person you hired and end this shit!" Angel yelled, plunging the cell in Keaton's face.

"It doesn't work like that. We place the hit with a third party, put the money in an untraceable account and the money is transferred once the job is complete. There is never any direct contact. That way all parties are protected," Keaton explained.

"Are you telling me my father is going to die and there is nothing I can do about it?"

"Yes, that's what I'm telling you. I'm sorry, Angel."

"You should be," Angel said, right before emptying her clip on Keaton. She sprayed his chest with bullets before putting one in the head to guarantee he was dead.

Chapter Six

Dirty Laundry

When Dominique touched down in Miami she was not ready for the endless amount of glistening skin floating around in her face. You would think since she worked at a strip club that she would be used to the scantily clad bodies strolling down Ocean Drive but nope. Seeing tits and ass jiggling around in a dimly lit club was in stark contrast to seeing it prancing around in broad daylight.

Desmond had a driver pick her up from the airport and on the ride to the hotel, in the heart of Miami Beach, Dominique got an eyeful. Women of all shapes, sizes, and color were walking down the street like it was their own personal beach runway except there was no sand. Instead, there was an endless amount of restaurants and hotels.

All the eye candy decorating the streets intimated Dominique, but she didn't let that deter her. She wanted to stay focused on her goal. So instead of walking around in shame of the less than stellar clothes she packed in her suitcase, Dominique decided to ditch them.

"Before you take me to my hotel, can we stop at the store over there," Dominique said, pointing to a boutique that had a steady flow of attractive women going in and out.

"That won't be a problem. Do you need me to come in with you?"

"No, you can wait in the car, but thanks." Dominique opened her purse and looked at the wad of money Desmond had given her. She wanted to be careful on what she spent the money on since she had to pay him back every penny. But Dominique thought of the new clothes as an investment in her future. Not wasting any time to recoup his money, Desmond had Dominique scheduled to work that day. She wanted to make a bold statement her first night on a new stage and the shabby costumes she brought with her weren't going to cut it.

"I'll be parked right here. Take your time," the driver told Dominique.

"I won't be long." Dominique stepped out the car and closed the door. She eyed a showstopper prominently displayed in the store's front window. "Talk about winning." She smiled and headed inside.

Aspen sat on her bed going through her phone looking at old pictures with her and Laurie. She missed her friend and knew that she didn't have to die. Other than the earring and her gut instinct, Aspen didn't have proof that Taren was involved in Laurie's murder. She knew that wasn't enough, but didn't know how to get the evidence she needed.

There has to be a way to prove Taren's involvement in Laurie's death, but how? Wait... Taren admitted that she knew this Tony motherfucker. It's probably no coincidence that he assaulted

Laurie and Taren used to service him. Maybe if I investigate Tony's background, it will lead me to his connection with Taren because I think it's a lot more than just sex, Aspen thought to herself.

"Fuck! I need to start getting ready," Aspen said out loud looking at the time. All the girls were meeting with Angel's new partner today and she didn't want to be late. Aspen was looking forward to meeting the man who would be taking over the daily operation of Angel's Girls, but she also knew that Taren would be in attendance. It was becoming more and more difficult for Aspen to see her face. All it did was make her determined to bring Taren down. So instead of hopping in the shower, Aspen made a phone call first.

"Hey Clarissa, what you doing girl?"

"Getting ready for work."

"You still working over at Platinum Dolls?"

"Nah, I'm over at this new strip club and I don't want to be late because the owner is a real asshole," Clarissa complained.

"Then why you stripping there?"

"'Cause the money is right. Dude be having all the big spenders come through."

"'Nough said. I'm not gonna hold you up, but I got a question. Are you still cool with that one guy that does a lot of security at nightclubs?"

"Oh, you talkin' 'bout Rico. Yeah, that's my people. Why?"

"I don't know if you heard about this dude named Tony who was killed awhile ago. It was an article in the paper."

"Nah, I didn't hear about that. I don't really read the paper or watch the news." Clarissa laughed.

"Well, in the paper it said the dude did bodyguard, security work. I wanted to see if Rico knew him."

"If the nigga was on the scene then Rico definitely probably heard of him. He knows everybody."

"Girl, I need you to call him and ask him about a dude named Tony Marsh. Tell him he did security and got killed not too long ago and see what he tells you. I really need for you to do this for me, Clarissa," Aspen pleaded.

"You my people, I got you. I'ma call him when I get in the car on my way to work. If he don't answer I'll leave a message. He'll get back to me and when he does I'll hit you up. I promise."

"I love you, girl. Thank you!" Aspen beamed.

"Anything for you. We go way back. I'll call you later on. Love you, too. Bye! I gotta go!" Clarissa hung up and Aspen smiled.

"Please let Rico know something about this Tony character. He's the key to me connecting the dots to Taren and airing all her dirty laundry. I can feel it in my stomach," Aspen said out loud before getting in the shower.

When Angel strolled through the front door, Darien was sitting in the living room waiting for her. Angel's initial reaction was to ask him why he wasn't upstairs resting, but stopped herself.

"You're going to just walk past me and act like you don't see me sitting here?" Darien questioned in an aggravated tone. Angel ignored him, which made Darien speak louder. "Why the hell didn't you come home last night?!" Angel continued to keep walking so Darien followed behind her. He could barely keep up as he was still walking with a cane.

"Please stop following me," Angel said coldly.

"I know you're upset with me, but we're still married. You're my wife. You can't ignore me."

Angel headed up the stairs to the master bedroom. By the time Darien was able to get up there she had already taken out her suitcase and started packing.

"What are you doing?" there was panic in Darien's voice.

"I'm leaving."

"Leaving... where are you going?"

Angel stopped and for the first time since coming home she made eye contact with her husband. "I'm going to find my father."

"You're going to look for Nico?"

"He's my father... right." Angel stated through clenched teeth.

"You can stay here and look for Nico. I'll even have my men help you."

"Oh, how considerate of you, Darien. Too bad you didn't do that before I put a hit out on him," she seethed. "Don't even bother," Angel raised her hand and said before Darien could get a word in. "I'm sure you're well aware that the hit Keaton put out on Nico can't be stopped. So I need to find my father before it's too late."

"Listen, maybe there's something else Keaton can do. I've been trying to get in touch with him since yesterday, but he hasn't been answering his phone. Let me try again now."

"Don't waste your time. Keaton won't be answering your call now or later," Angel said and continued to pack her clothes.

"I don't understand, what do you mean by that?" Darien was baffled by his wife's comment. "Do you know why Keaton isn't answering his phone?"

"Yeah, because he's dead." Angel's reply was so aloof that it took a moment for it to register with Darien. Once it sunk in, he damn near fell to the floor.

"What did you say?" his voice was so low, Angel almost didn't hear the question. However, she did catch it, but chose not to respond. "Did you say Keaton is dead?" this time Darien asked in an audible tone.

"Yes, that's what I said."

"Are you sure... how do you know?"

"I'm positive because I killed him." Angel put her last item in her suitcase and began zipping it up."

"You killed Keaton." Darien's eyes watered up. If Angel had cared, she would've been over-whelmed by the excruciating pain her husband was in.

"It hurts doesn't it," she affirmed with ab-solutely no emotion. "Now you know how I feel. The pain you caused me by keeping me away from my father. Keaton allowed me to put a hit on my own flesh and blood. You really should die too, but then again you're basically dead anyway. You can barely walk, you're boxing career is now non-existent, so there's no need for me to put a bullet in your head like I did to Keaton." She smirked with so much coldness that Darien was actually afraid of his own wife.

"What have you done?" he mumbled in shock and horror.

"You should be asking yourself that question. What have you done? You're the reason why Keaton is dead and you're the reason this marriage is over."

"You don't mean that. I know you still love me, Angel."

Angel laughed and continued to laugh. "You still love me after I killed your best friend… the man who was like a brother to you."

"Of course I do. You're right, it is my fault. I should've told you the truth." Darien sat down on the bed as if defeated. "I let my anger for Nico cloud my judgment. I'm hurt about Keaton, but you're my wife and I love you, Angel. I love you more than anything in this world. I don't have anything left, but you. Please don't leave me. Don't give up on us."

Darien appeared to be a broken man and his

heartfelt plea did move Angel, but her anger over being kept in the dark about Nico was stronger. "I can't make you any promises right now, Darien."

"Can you at least promise me that you'll give this marriage a chance before ending it?"

"I can't even consider staying in this marriage until I locate Nico. If I'm not able to warn him about the hit before he's killed, not only is this marriage over, but you'll be spending the rest of your life watching your back."

After Angel said her peace, she grabbed her suitcase and left, resolute that she would unite with her father or die trying.

Chapter Seven

Reunited

"Damn that nigga fine!" Monique whispered in excitement to Taren when Desmond came into the room. "You think that's Angel's new business partner?"

"I have no idea, but I'm assuming since he showed up, it's a good possibility," Taren replied.

"I hope not 'cause he so fine, I might just let him keep all my money." Monique giggled, crushing hard on her new boss.

"Good afternoon. My name is Desmond Blackwell and I'm Angel's new partner. She has spoken highly of each of you and I'm looking forward to working with you ladies."

"I'm sure I speak for everyone when I say that we're all looking forward to working with you too, Mr. Blackwell," Amber said.

"Call me Desmond." He smiled.

"Desmond, as I was saying, we're looking forward to working with you too, but before we continue, shouldn't we wait for Angel. I know she's supposed to be here also."

"Gosh, Amber is always so far up Angel's ass," Taren mumbled, rolling her eyes.

"You're right. Angel was supposed to be here today, but an unexpected family emergency came up so she won't be able to make it. But trust me, you're in good hands. If Angel didn't agree, I wouldn't be standing here." Desmond gave the ladies another million dollar smile and all the women smiled back. All of them except for Taren.

This nigga coming in here with his designer suit, iced out, cheesing, got these chicks ready to drop their panties. Acting like he such a gentleman and shit. I bet that motherfucker ain't nobody nice, Taren thought to herself. *And what's up with Angel and all these family emergencies. Something heavy is going on with her and I need to find out what it is.*

"So ladies I just wanted to introduce myself. I'm sure you all need to get ready for work so I won't keep you. But if you have any questions or concerns, don't hesitate to let me know. I want Angel's Girls to continue to be a successful business," Desmond said, giving the women one final look at his perfect teeth.

That wasn't enough for some of the women. They quickly ran up to Desmond to personally introduce themselves, including Monique. Taren observed from her chair also taking an opportunity to keep an eye on Aspen. She had been keeping her distance since their confrontation at her apartment. Taren wondered if Aspen believed her and left the altercation in the past or if she was still harboring resentment. *There's only one way to find out what's going on with Aspen,* Taren thought to herself before heading over to speak to her.

"Aspen, hey! How are you?" Taren used an extra chipper voice as if the two were besties.

"Hey, Taren! It's so good to see you," Aspen put on an equally chipper voice, even standing up to hug Taren. "I miss hanging out with you. How have you been?"

"I've been doing okay. Getting used to being back at work. It's a little difficult. Laurie has been so heavy on my mind."

"I know what you mean, but Laurie would want us to enjoy our lives. Of course we'll never forget her, but she wouldn't want us to spend all of our time mourning her either," Aspen said.

"You're right. I know it's been especially hard for you since the two of you were so close. It's good to know that you're moving forward though."

"Yes. I know that's what Laurie would want. So what do you think of our new boss?" Aspen asked, changing the subject.

Taren glanced over at the circle of women still clamoring for Desmond's attention. "He seems to be very popular."

"Yes, he does. I can't lie, he is one delectable piece of chocolate. I wonder how Angel met him."

"She said he came highly recommended and knows a lot of major players. Didn't she mention he owned a lot of high-end strip clubs?"

"That's right. Angel did say that. Well, I'm sure he has a long list of clientele that will keep us very busy. Speaking of clients, let me get out of here as I have one to meet in less than an hour. Call me. Let's do drinks soon." Aspen kissed Taren on the cheek and left.

Taren was beaming with confidence as she watched Aspen exit the room. *I guess that show I put on for Aspen worked perfectly. She no longer thinks I had anything to do with Laurie's death. That's a relief because if I had to kill her too, people might start getting suspicious. Luckily, it's no longer a concern.* Believing her and Aspen were once again cool put Taren in a great mood. So much so she decided to be a part of the Desmond fan club, joining the other women surrounding him.

Aspen couldn't get in her car fast enough when she realized she missed Clarissa's call. "Pick up the phone!" she hissed out loud when it kept ringing with no answer. When it went to voice-mail, Aspen kept calling back until she saw a text message come through.

About to go on stage. Will call you after my set. I got some info for you.

"OMG! I knew my girl would come through." Aspen smiled, speeding off.

Angel was in her hotel suite waiting for room

service to be delivered when her cell began to vibrate. It was from an unknown number, but she had a good idea who it was. "Hello."

"Angel, glad you answered."

"I've been waiting for your call. Tell me you have news."

"Very good news. I located Nico Carter."

"Where is he? I can go online and book my flight right now."

"You don't have to. He's right here in Miami," the private investigator informed Angel.

"Are you serious?!"

"Yes. I can text you the address or you can write it down."

"Do both. Go head, I have a pen." Angel wrote down the address as she became flooded with excitement at the idea of seeing her father.

"Angel, you didn't stipulate why you wanted me to track this man down, but he seems to be quite powerful. He constantly surrounds himself with armed security. Not sure what business he's in, but whatever it is you need to be careful."

"I will and thank you so much for getting on top of this so quickly."

"My pleasure. Plus, you pay extremely well so that helps." He chuckled. "Always a pleasure working with you, Angel."

"Same here… thanks again." Angel rushed the private investigator off the phone, cancelled room service, grabbed her purse, and headed out. She wanted to see her father. Everything else could wait.

Angel pressed down hard on the gas pedal of her sequin blue Bentley Continental GT V8 S, wanting to get the maximum engine output from the 582 horsepower. She even ran a couple of red lights in a quest to get to her father. She had no idea how long he would be at his current location, since based on the address and information the private investigator texted her, it was a club or lounge of some sort. It was late afternoon so Angel figured Nico had to be at the spot for business purposes. When she finally arrived there were only three cars in the parking lot and one was pulling off. Angel parked her car and practically ran to the front door.

"Excuse me, Miss, but you can't go in there," a security guard said putting his hand up to stop Angel from coming inside. "This establishment is closed for business and won't be open to the public until later on this evening."

"I understand, but I'm here to see Nico Carter. It's very important that I speak to him."

"There's a closed meeting going on in there

and they can't be disturbed."

"Tell him that Angel Riviera is here to see him. Please! Just go tell Nico that," she pleaded.

The security guard gave Angel a menacing stare, but she showed no signs of fearing him. He then glanced over at the car she arrived in, before once again staring at her, but this time he started from the bottom and worked his way up to the top. "You say your name is Angel?" he questioned.

"Yes! Angel Riviera."

"A'ight, Angel. You stay right here. I'll be back."

"Okay! I'll be right here," she said anxiously.

The security guard went inside. Angel was tempted to run in behind him, but she quickly noticed that he closed and locked the door. "Please see me, Nico," Angel said out loud, rubbing her hands together nervously. As she waited it felt like an eternity. Her nerves were so wound up she barely heard her phone ringing. "I have nothing to say to you, Darien," Angel scoffed, pressing the decline button on her cell.

A few minutes later the door finally opened and dread swooped down on Angel. She feared the security officer was coming to tell her that Nico didn't want to see her. Not wanting to face the sadness that would ensue from being rejected by her father, Angel was tempted to turn around and walk away.

"Here I was looking for you and you found me," Nico said after he opened the door and came outside. Nico's face didn't have much of an expression, but his eyes were beaming and smiled for him. "Are you going to stand there or come give your father a hug?"

Angel ran to Nico as he embraced her with open arms. "I'm so sorry. I didn't know you were my father. I came looking for you the moment I found out," Angel cried.

"It's okay. I prayed we would find each other and we have. That's all that matters," Nico said holding Angel tightly. "I've dreamt of this moment as soon as I found out that you were my daughter."

"How did you even know?"

"For one, you look so much like your mother and then when I saw the birthmark on the back of your neck. I have the same birthmark. Very rare."

"Wow! That's amazing. I guess it worked out for the best that you had me kidnapped." Angel laughed.

"I wish I hadn't found you under those circumstances, but if it brought us together then yes, it did work out." Nico chuckled. "Why don't you come inside so we can sit down and talk some more."

"That would be great! Let me just get something from my car. It's a little gift I got you." Angel smiled.

"You didn't have to do that."

"I wanted to." Angel blushed. "I'll be right back."

"I'll be here waiting." Nico watched proudly as Angel went to her car. He knew she had it tough growing up, but even with all she had endured, there was a sweetness about Angel that made Nico love her instantly.

"I hope you love this," Angel said reaching over on the passenger seat and getting the gift-wrapped present. She rushed back to Nico, excited for him to see what she got. He stood waiting and they exchanged smiles, as Angel got closer. But like all fairytales, doom was lurking in the shadows. Angel was the first to notice a white man, dressed in khakis, a short sleeve navy shirt, baseball cap, and a lightweight full zip jacket with sunglasses. He was clothed to blend effortlessly with a crowd. He had a very non-threatening style, so non-threatening that he would fall under the radar and go unnoticed and that's what made him stand out to Angel.

Nico could see that something or someone had caught Angel's attention. He turned in the direction she was staring and that's when they both saw the man unzip his coat and pull out a Ruger .22 with an integral suppressor. "Watch out!" Angel shrieked, sprinting towards Nico and jumping in front of him to be his shield. As the assassin released his bullets, Nico shoved Angel to the ground and leaned over her before getting lit up.

A few seconds later, two of Nico's security came up with their own weapons and sprayed an endless round of bullets in the assassin's direction. The man fell to the ground, lying in a pool of blood only a few feet away from Angel and Nico.

A deafening silence hovered in the air after the ringing of bullets stopped. "Nico," Angel called out in an unknowing tone, but she got no reply. She then started saying his name louder and louder until she felt the security men lifting his body off of her.

"Call 911! He needs to be airlifted to the nearest hospital ASAP!" one of the guards yelled out. The security guard then started performing CPR, but he was getting nothing.

"No! No! No! This can't be happening!" Angel wailed. "Please save my father! Pleaaaaaaase!" she cried out to God.

Chapter Eight

Star Power

Dominique arrived to Diamond & Pearls strip club ready to make her debut. She pulled her mid back length jet black hair into a tight bun and covered it with a reddish brown long deep wave full lace wig. She had become somewhat of a makeup expert from watching YouTube gurus so her face was beat. The other ladies were shading the fuck out of the new girl but Dominique paid them dust. She came to show up and show out.

"You're up next," one of the hostesses at the club told her. Dominique wasn't used to working in such a professional environment. Desmond ran a top-notch, classy club. Everyone from the waitresses, bartenders, strippers, and staff in general conducted themselves like they were working at a five star hotel instead of jiggling ass for dollars.

"Thanks." Dominique grinned, eyeing herself in the grand silver three-sided, full-length mirror. She knew she was winning in her new millennium version of I Dream Of Jeannie getup. The turquoise sparkling translux light skirt with matching thong and bra had her shining bright like a diamond, even in a strip club full of eye candy.

When Dominique heard the DJ announce her name and the music emanating from the speakers getting louder, she sashayed on the stage like she owned it. She had him play Show Stopper by Danity Kane. Dominique figured it would be the perfect song for her debut.

"Who in the hell does this hussy think she is," Nesa, one of the strippers, commented to Clarissa. As both women watched Dominique bumping and grinding across the stage. When she slithered effortlessly like a slimy snake up and down the pole both women shook their heads. Customers weren't making it rain on Dominique, it was a full fledge storm. Her petite, yet voluptuous toned body had all the boys and some girls going crazy.

"Can't lie, she's pretty dope," Clarissa admitted. "Is she new because I've never worked a shift with her. But I haven't been working here that long."

"Yeah, she's new. This is her first night. One of the other girls told me she's a transport from either Arkansas, Alabama… one of those places that start with an A." Nesa shrugged.

"How did she end up in Miami?" Clarissa wanted to know.

"Supposedly the boss man himself found her in some rundown strip club and brought her ass up here. I wish he would've left her right where she was at. We don't need no extra competition."

"Stop worrying. There's enough money coming through the doors for all of us to eat good."

"Humph, if you say so. Personally, I think we already overstaffed. I don't need to share my coins wit' no more bitches. No offense to you." Nesa winked, folding her arms.

"No offense taken, but it looks like we don't have a choice so be nice." Clarissa smirked. "Gotta go, I'm up next." When Clarissa passed Dominique as she came off the stage, she decided to give her some words of encouragement. "Great job!"

"Thank you!" Dominique wasn't expecting the compliment since most of the ladies had been giving her the cold shoulder. She was thrilled that at least one girl was trying to make her feel welcomed. On her way to freshen up before going back on stage she noticed the hostess making a beeline in her direction.

"Mr. Blackwell would like to see you in his office. I'll show you the way," the hostess said dryly. Dominique stepped up her pace to keep up with the woman who seemed to be in a rush. She took her down a hall that Dominique didn't even know existed. The office door was open as if Desmond had been waiting for her to arrive.

"Thank you, Tori. That's all for now. Come have a seat, Dominique," Desmond said, closing the door before taking a seat behind his desk.

"What a nice office, but I shouldn't be surprised based on how nice the club is," Dominique said.

"Thank you, but I didn't have you brought in here to discuss décor. I wanted to find out how are things going so far?"

"Everything is cool. I've only danced once, but so far so good."

"From what I saw on the monitor, things seem to be going great."

"I'm glad you think so... that's a relief. You seemed a bit icy so I wasn't sure if I had done something wrong."

"No, you haven't done anything wrong. You seem to be doing everything right. I see you took my advice and polished up your look. I like your new attire."

"Glad you approve. It was a tad bit pricey, but based on the amount of money I collected after my performance, I think it was a wise investment."

"I agree. Your attire is just as important as the body that's in it. The clientele that comes through these doors want to be visually stimulated first. You have to present yourself like a well-packaged gift that they'll pay any amount of money to unwrap."

"I like that analogy. Hopefully, it will work for me."

"It already has. One of my important customers asked to get a private dance with you."

"Really?!"

"Yes. He watched your performance on stage and was impressed. Your package was correct and now he wants to spend."

"So how much will he spend for a private dance?

"Minimum fifteen hundred."

"Wow! Are you fuckin' joking?"

"I never joke about money. But remember I told you, I had no doubt you would make me back all my money your first night working."

"How did you know?"

"This is what I do. If you listen to what I tell you and follow my rules, I'll make you a rich young lady."

As Dominique listened to Desmond her mind marveled to just how rich she could be. Then she wondered if working at an upscale strip club like Diamond & Pearls could lead to even bigger opportunities, like she heard other former strippers brag about.

"Are you listening to what I'm saying, Dominique?" Desmond questioned, as it appeared her mind had drifted off.

"I'm listening to every word. I guess I'm having dreams of being a star." Dominique laughed.

"Hey, you never know. I see star power in you."

"Fo' real!" Dominique's eyes widened.

"Yes. But if that's what you really want, start mentally preparing yourself now. Always remember the bigger the star, the bigger the problems."

Aspen woke up on her living room sofa after falling asleep waiting for Clarissa's call. She reached over on the table to grab her cell and saw there were no missed calls from her friend. She was about to text her when her phone began ringing.

"Girl, I've been waiting for you to call me all night," Aspen said when she answered the call.

"Sorry about that. I was mad busy at work and didn't get off until late," Clarissa explained.

"I'm guessing you made some good money."

"I did, but a bitch got a lot of bills so I needed every dollar."

"I feel you. I'm working nonstop for the next couple weeks so I can get caught up." Aspen sighed, looking at the stack of bills piling up on her kitchen counter.

"You can always come work part time at the strip club. The owner seems to be on the lookout for new talent," Clarissa joked.

"Don't tempt me. But Angel has a new partner and he's supposed to amp business all the way up. But we'll see."

"Word. Maybe I need to come work over there part time…. shoooot. But I don't think I can sell no pussy."

"Bitch, what you think you doing when you on that stage at the strip club and grinding all up on niggas. You selling pussy just like me it's just dry sex."

Both women burst out laughing. "You crazy!" Clarissa continued to laugh.

"I know. Don't pay me no mind. But you know what I wanted to ask you. Who is the owner of the new club you working at?"

"Ummm, Desmond Blackwell."

"I knew it! Girl, why is his fine ass Angel's new business partner!" Aspen exclaimed.

"Get the fuck outta here! Talk about a small world. He is fine, but he is super anal. When I first started working he was smiling and shit. Showing off his pretty ass teeth, but after a week or so he became a complete asshole. Don't know how he acting with you all, but don't get fooled by his good looks and charm. That man is straight business," Clarissa warned.

"Humph, thanks for the heads up, but umm enough about Desmond. Tell me what you found out from your friend Rico."

"Girl, you got me talking about so much other shit I almost forgot why I called you in the first place. So yeah, Rico did know that Tony dude. He said they were mad cool."

"Get out!"

"Yeah, he said Tony even tried to bring him in on some deal he was working on."

"What deal?" Aspen questioned.

"Not sure. Honestly I didn't ask. He did tell me that Tony worked for some major drug kingpin, but Tony was trying to get a side business going."

"Interesting. Do you think I can talk to Rico? I want to ask him a few questions myself."

"Yeah, but I think you should let me go with you. Rico can be a tad standoffish to people he don't know, but he's comfortable around me so he won't have no problem running off at the mouth."

"Bet... say no more. When do you have time to meet up with him? I really need to speak to him as soon as possible."

"Let me call him and find out when and where is good for him, then I'll hit you back."

"Cool! Thanks so much, Clarissa. This Rico dude might have the information I need," Aspen said, itching to get closer at bringing Taren down.

Chapter Nine

Back On Top

Precious and Aaliyah held hands during their flight to Miami. Justina and Amir were in the seats across from them. Aaliyah appreciated having her two best friends come with her, but it was her mother's support she needed the most.

"I can't believe they couldn't give you any other information other than he'd been shot," Aaliyah said, glancing out the window, staring into the clouds.

"I know. They were prepping your father for emergency surgery right before we got on the plane. We won't know anything else until we get to the hospital," Precious told her daughter.

"What if he doesn't make it through surgery?"

"Aaliyah, don't think like that."

"It's true. We don't know. There is a real possibility that he won't survive his injuries. I just pray Dad is able to hold on until we make it. If he does die, I want us to be by his side. We've already lost grandfather, I don't want to lose my father too."

"Nico, is not going to die. I've known that man most of my adult life and it's going to take more than some bullets to take your father out." Precious wanted to console Aaliyah if at all possible.

"The most important thing right now is for Daddy to survive. After that, we need to focus on finding the person who did this so we can take them out," Aaliyah stated before gazing back out at the clouds.

Angel thought she was going to have a nervous breakdown right there in the middle of the hospital. It made her have flashbacks to being in the hospital in Hawaii on her wedding night, praying that her husband wouldn't die. The night was the turning point in her life. She set all of this in motion during one of the darkest moments in her life. Now Angel had to accept that because of her decision, Nico was now fighting for his life. That realization made her loathe her husband so when she noticed he was calling her, Angel was tempted to throw her phone across the building, but instead she answered.

"What is it, Darien?"

"I can't believe I'm hearing your voice. You've been ignoring my calls for days."

"The only reason I answered was because I wanted you to know that my father is in surgery right now fighting for his life."

"What! Angel, I'm so sorry. What happened?"

"What the fuck do you think happened! And spare me with the sorry shit. It's your fuckin' fault that any of this happened in the first place."

"Angel, I was wrong for not telling you that Nico was your father, but I did and I still do think he was the one that had me shot."

"I don't fuckin' care!" she yelled into the phone. "If I knew Nico was my father, I wouldn't of put a hit on him whether he had you shot or not. That's my father you sonofabitch! Do you think I would kill the man that gave me life for you? Because of your selfishness, you might've deprived me from ever having a relationship with my dad. If Nico dies, I'll never forgive you, Darien. Never!" Angel shouted, not caring who in the hospital heard her.

"Angel, baby I promise I'll make this right. Please believe how sorry I am, but I'll make it right." All Darien heard was silence after Angel ended the call. "Damn you Nico!" he hollered, slamming his phone down on the bed. When the phone hit the silk comforter, it slid down to the floor. Darien looked around for his cane and noticed it was across the bedroom by the chair. He was about to call out to his homecare provider, but remembered one of his bodyguards took her to the grocery store to get some things he needed.

"Fuck it!" Darien said, slowly standing up. He held onto the edge of the bed while he tried to maintain his balance. "I got this." Darien sighed in relief once he took a couple steps towards his phone without any issues. After the fourth step, his knees buckled beneath him and Darien fell face first on the Calcutta gold stone floor. He howled out in pain, but there was no one there to help him.

Darien was laying on the floor for what seemed like hours to him, but it was the feeling of helplessness that made time stand still. "I can't go on like this," Darien looked up at the ceiling and said. His body was numb from being weak, but he was determined to reach his phone. He began to crawl inch by inch. When he finally got ahold of his cell, there was only one call he wanted to make.

"Hello."

"Hey, it's me Blaze."

"I know your number. I know who this is. I'd be lying if I didn't say I'm surprised you called me after out last conversation."

"I know I said I was done with boxing and I didn't need you anymore, but I was wrong. I need you more than ever," Darien admitted to Reggie, his long time coach.

"Where is this coming from? Just last week when I was begging you to let me help you with your physical therapy so we could work towards getting you back in the gym, you damn near hung up the phone on me."

"I know, but I'm stuck on this floor right now feeling like an infant. I don't wanna live like this. Not only do I want my strength back, but I want to stay champ."

"It ain't gon' be easy and I'm not gonna coddle you," Reggie stated.

"I know this, that's why I called you because you're the only person that can put me back on top. I can't let what happened to me make me give up and become a burden on my people."

"Are you talking about your wife right now?" Reggie asked.

"Angel is the motivation. We going through something serious and I don't know if we're gonna make it. What I do know is I gotta get my mind and body right if I stand a fighting chance to save my marriage."

"Then we betta get to work. I'll see you tomorrow morning," Reggie decided.

"I'll be ready." After their call ended, Darien still sat on his bedroom floor unable to stand up or get to his cane. While he waited for his caregiver and bodyguard to return he used the time to reflect on his predicament. A few months ago Darien was on top of the world. He was preparing for the fight of his life and for his wedding with the love of his life. Overnight, he lost both, but Darien was willing to do anything to get them both back.

Chapter 10

Who The F&@! Are You

"Who the fuck are you and why are you sitting next to my father?!" Aaliyah barked when she stepped into Nico's hospital room.

Angel glanced up to see two women standing by the door. She was holding Nico's hand and debated on whether she should let it go or keep it close to her heart. She was having a private moment with her father that had now come to an abrupt end.

"I'll leave you alone with your dad," Angel said wanting to keep the peace.

"You're not going anywhere until you tell me who the hell you are," Aaliyah stood blocking the entrance with her arms crossed.

"Aaliyah, don't get yourself worked up," Precious advised her daughter.

"Nah. We come here to see my father and some random chick sitting at his bedside, holding his hand like she wifey or some shit. She got some explainin' to do," Aaliyah popped.

"First of all, I'm not some random chick, so you can go ahead and remove that from your vocabulary when speaking to me," Angel said point blank.

Aaliyah was dumbfounded that this unknown chick had the audacity to speak up for herself and she wasn't having it. "You might think you some hot shit 'cause you the flavor of the moment for my father, but he'll neva.." Aaliyah rolled her neck extra hard. "Approve of you speaking to me like this."

"Is that right." Angel gave Aaliyah an 'I don't give a fuck' stare. Precious couldn't help but detect that something was amiss. The young lady standing in front of them was way too comfortable in her position, but Precious couldn't figure out why.

"What did you say your name was again?" Precious questioned.

"I didn't say."

"Don't be gettin' smart wit' my mother!" Aaliyah yelled.

"You need to calm down. Your father just got out of surgery and he's resting. The last thing he needs is chaos in his room. Furthermore, I wasn't getting smart with your mother. I was simply stating the obvious... I never told you my name."

"Listen you hussy. I don't know who the fuck you think you talkin' to but don't come at us like that. We belong here and you don't. So get yo' shit and go," Aaliyah demanded.

"Out of respect for Nico I'll go, but I will be back."

"Oh no the hell you won't!" Aaliyah spit.

"Yes, I will. Because when your father wakes up, he'll be asking for me. Then you'll know my name," Angel stated with cynicism and walked out the hospital room.

"That was bizarre," Precious said, baffled by the dialogue that transpired.

"Yeah, it was!" Aaliyah exclaimed, taking a seat where Angel had just been sitting next to Nico. "The nerve of that girl. I know Daddy was devastated when you ended the marriage, but what is he thinking getting involved with someone that young. I mean she's my age, maybe even younger. If that gold digger thinks she's about to make a come up off my father she's sorely mistaken," Aaliyah scoffed.

"We can deal with her later. The important thing is Nico made it out of surgery and the doctor said he'll pull through." Precious sighed.

"Of course I'm grateful my father is going to be okay, but I know seeing that girl holding Daddy's hand when we walked in bothered you."

"It bothered me, but not for the reasons you might think. I'm very happy and more in love than ever with Supreme."

"I know you're in love with Daddy. I didn't mean it that way." Aaliyah shook her head. "I know you still care about him and you would never want some young bimbo taking advantage."

"Nico is far from stupid. He's run across more than enough bimbos in his life and none of them have taken advantage of him. Trust me, I know."

"Then why do you think that silly chick seemed so overly confident with herself? As if she had some unbreakable bond with him and what's between her legs is gold. She had no concern that we were his family, not her."

"In fairness, Aaliyah, you were a tad bit abrasive when we first walked in. I could see that making her a little defensive," Precious acknowledged.

"Are you seriously taking her side?"

"No, I'm not taking her side. I'm always team Aaliyah and I would never admit any of this in front of her. But we're alone and I'm being honest."

"So you think I was out of line?"

"If I was dating a man and his daughter walked in the room and the first thing she said was, who the fuck are you, I would be pissed. Honestly, she handled it better than me. But then again, my temper is legendary." Precious laughed.

"Maybe you're right, but I can't help but be protective of Daddy, especially after that Ashley/Tori fiasco. I still blame myself for prepping her to seduce my father."

"Aaliyah, that wasn't your fault. You had no idea she was being used to infiltrate your father's business."

"I know, but I never want anything like that

to happen to him again. Even though he would never admit it, he was deeply hurt."

"Of course he was, anybody would be, but he bounced back because he's Nico Carter," Precious said, stroking the side of Nico's face. "Whoever this girl is, that was probably the first and last time you'll ever see her face. She'll have absolutely no impact on your life so stop worrying."

Precious wanted to believe her own words for her daughter's sake, but deep down something was making her feel uneasy. She couldn't figure out what or why so instead she brushed it off. Nico was alive and for now that was all that mattered.

"What a snobby bitch!" Angel fumed, tossing her purse down on the bed when she got back to her hotel room. She had been cursing Aaliyah out since leaving the hospital and although a full hour had passed, she hadn't stopped. "Yes!" she answered the phone loudly.

"Mrs. Blaze, I'm sorry to disturb you," the man working the front desk said politely. "I wasn't sure if you noticed the light flashing on

"I get that, but what do you want me to do? I had nothing to do with Laurie's death."

"Then you need to find out who did so the police can stop sniffing around you. The longer Laurie's murder goes unsolved the more reason the cops have to investigate you and our business. So handle that. If you don't think you can, then let me put my men on it."

"Let me see what I can find out first. If I need your assistance then I'll let you know. Is there anything else?"

"Not right now. But Angel, remember we're partners now, so we're in this together. Don't forget that."

"Thanks, Desmond. I'll talk to you soon," Angel said ending the call slightly aggravated. She couldn't decide if her new partner meant well or if he was an overbearing asshole. What she couldn't deny was Desmond had a point. They didn't need the police sniffing around. She couldn't wait around for the cops to do their job. Angel had to find out who the killer was so she could not only get justice for Laurie, but get the case closed once and for all.

Chapter Eleven

Baby Girl

"Justina, if you could've seen that arrogant bitch. She thought she was such hot shit. I can't believe my father would get involved with someone that young," Aaliyah huffed. "She was even wearing these black Tom Ford caged open-toe, velvet, lace up booties, with the gold metal tip on the heels. I've been eyeing those too."

"Yeah, I know what shoe you're talking about. Super sexy." Justina nodded.

"They're like twenty-four hundred dollars. I know my father must've bought them for her. As if she could afford them on her own. What a leech," Aaliyah spat in frustration.

"So how serious are they?"

"Not sure. I haven't been able to talk to my dad about it. Every time I've gone to visit him at the hospital he's sleeping. He's woken up a couple of times, but it's only briefly, so I haven't been able to grill him about her. I don't even know her freakin' name," Aaliyah scoffed, pushing away her plate of fresh fruit.

"Wow, this chick has really gotten under your skin."

"Is it that obvious," Aaliyah said sarcastically. My mother said I shouldn't worry, that she's probably some passing fling, but she was so cocky. Not so much of what she said but her attitude, very flippant like. Fingers crossed my mom is right and I'll never have to see her face again." Aaliyah took a sip of her Bellini not able to get the mystery woman off her mind.

"So how much longer are you going to stay in Miami?" Justina questioned wanting to change the subject.

"Probably for awhile. You know Dale lives here and we'll be married soon so it will be my home too. I hope you're not leaving already?! It's nice having my bestie here."

"No, no, no. I'll stay for as long as you need me. Plus, Miami is pretty nice and I'm loving the beaches. So no, I have no plans of leaving anytime soon. You're stuck with me." Justina smiled.

"Great, but I know Amir's ready for you to get back to New York."

"He is, but I wanted to be here for you. He understands so Amir is coming here!"

"What! That's awesome. It will be like old times all three of us hanging out. As soon as my father gets better, we have to hit the streets. Miami has some of the best nightclubs."

"Sounds like a plan. We have to squeeze some shopping in there too."

"No doubt! I feel like going right now, but I'm supposed to be meeting my mom at the hospital," Aaliyah said looking at her watch. "I need to be going. Maybe we can go tomorrow."

"Let's do it."

"I know I haven't been a very good host, but try to make yourself at home."

"Aaliyah, I'm fine. Plus your condo is right here on the beach. I have no complaints. Go be with your dad. I have a few things I need to take care of anyway. But tomorrow we will be going shopping," Justina beamed.

"For sure. I'll see you later on when I get home. Call me if you need me!"

"You do the same." Justina waved goodbye to Aaliyah until she was out the door. "Thank gosh she's gone. I swear she's the same self-centered brat she's always been," Justina mumbled on her way outside to stand on the balcony. She relished in the amazing Miami skyline view. There didn't appear to be a cloud in sight. With the afternoon agile breeze and the calm sound of waves, it enabled Justina to think in peace.

Unfortunately, all she thought about was bringing Aaliyah down. *Typical Aaliyah. She only wishes happiness for herself. She's even praying that the new relationship her father's in will crash and burn. Gosh, I hope that whoever this woman is in his life sticks around for a long time simply to make Aaliyah miserable. In her mind there is only room for one other woman in her dad's life and that's her mother. The nerve of her, but if I have my way, none of this will end well for Aaliyah. All I need to do, is figure out the perfect way, to let Dale find out that Supreme is the one that killed his brother. That will surely destroy her engagement and knock Aaliyah off her high horse. But that's only the beginning,* Justina thought to herself as she let the sun beam down on her bare skin.

"Nico, I'm so happy you're finally awake and not dozing in and out." Precious smiled, squeezing Nico's hand.

"Maybe I need to get shot more often if that means waking up to you." Nico gave a slight grin before reaching for some water.

"I can get that." Precious grabbed the plastic pitcher and poured Nico a glass of water. It was the first time since she had visited him that he was showing signs of being back to his normal self.

"Where's Angel, is she okay?" Nico asked after quickly gulping down his water and pouring himself another glass.

"Do you mean Aaliyah?" Precious questioned thinking maybe Nico's cognitive functions were a little off after still recovering from the surgery.

"Woman, I ain't lost my damn mind. I know the difference between Aaliyah and Angel." Nico frowned.

"Well then who in the hell is Angel... oh that must be the woman that was at your bedside the first day Aaliyah and I got here."

"I'm sure it was. That must mean she wasn't hurt during the shooting. Thank God." Nico sighed in relief.

"Angel was with you when you got shot?'

"Yes, she was and I want her here with me now."

"Wow, this Angel woman must be special."

"She is. Very special."

"Nico, I know we're no longer married and I have no right to get involved in your personal life. However, I do consider us to be very good friends, friends that can discuss anything," Precious said with caution.

"We have always maintained a honest relationship with each other."

"Glad you think so. Then you won't get offended when I say that Angel is way too young for you. I think you're setting yourself up for a lot of headaches and heartaches jumping into a relationship with someone her age." Precious waited for Nico to say something, but instead he started laughing. "Ummm what is so funny?"

"You! I appreciate your concern, Precious, but..."

"Daddy, you're awake!" Aaliyah beamed, storming into the room before Nico could complete his sentence.

"Look at my baby girl! Come give your old man a hug."

"Daddy, I was so worried about you!" Aaliyah held onto her dad. "It might be time for you to change your lifestyle. I won't be able to sleep if I think every time you walk out the house you might get shot and where was your security? They can't be slippin' like that," Aaliyah belted becoming heated.

"Calm down. The situation was handled. Things can always go wrong I don't care what lifestyle you're living," Nico countered.

"Maybe, but we can't afford to have incidents like this happen again. Daddy, you know I lost grandfather, I can't lose you too."

"You won't baby girl. Your father is Teflon tough," Nico reassured his daughter and kissed her on the cheek.

"I tried to tell Aaliyah that it would take much more than a bullet to bring you down," Precious stated, grateful that Aaliyah was with her father and she could stop worrying.

"Daddy, did Mom have a chance to tell you about that woman that was here when we first came to visit you?"

"I actually did and your father told me how important the woman is to him," Precious said, hoping that would discourage Aaliyah from giving her father the third degree, but of course it didn't.

"Important... that woman is important to you, Daddy?"

"Yes, she is."

"Why is she important to you? How long have you even known her? It can't be that long. You and Mom were married up until a few months ago when you got a divorce."

"Aaliyah, don't bombard your father with all these questions. We really should let him rest."

"Precious, I'm fine. I've had more than enough rest. I'm ready to get the hell outta this place. I've never liked hospitals. I had to visit you in them one too many times."

"You have a point." Precious smirked.

"That's cute and everything, but let's stay on track," Aaliyah jumped in and said. "So answer the questions regarding this chick."

"Aaliyah, she has a name." Nico gave Aaliyah a stiff stare that she wasn't used to seeing from her father. "Which is Angel."

"How long have you been seeing this Angel person and isn't she a little bit too young for you? You must realize she's a gold digger, Daddy." Aaliyah would not let up.

"Despite what you and your mother might think, Angel isn't my girlfriend."

Precious and Aaliyah both looked at each other with confusion. "Then who is she?" mother and daughter asked simultaneously.

"Angel is my daughter," Nico stated proudly.

"You're what!" Aaliyah questioned loudly.

"Did you say your daughter?" Precious was more in disbelief.

"Yes. It's a long story, but I've finally been reunited with my baby girl."

"I'm your baby girl!" Aaliyah snapped becoming territorial.

"Aaliyah, you'll always be my baby girl. I meant that Angel was my youngest child. You're her big sister."

"No the hell I'm not!" Aaliyah folded her arms warily.

"Why are you acting like that? I thought you would be happy to have another sibling," Nico said sadly.

"I'm straight on that. I have Xavier. I don't need anymore siblings."

"Aaliyah," Precious said placing her hand on her daughter's arm. "Let's all relax. Before we get worked up, Nico, are you positive Angel is your daughter? I mean you would be a good mark. A wealthy man like you."

"Angel doesn't need my money. She runs her own business and she's married to Darien Blaze."

"The boxer?!" Aaliyah needed that clarified.

"Yes, the boxer. We all know he's extremely rich. So Angel doesn't need my money. Besides, I went looking for her after having a DNA test done."

"This all sounds so unbelievable. What made you even have a DNA test done?" Precious questioned still trying to wrap her mind around the fact that Nico had another grown daughter she knew nothing about for all these years.

"Like I said, it's a long story, but when I met her she had this birthmark on the back of her neck."

"The same birthmark you have on the back of yours," Precious was able to finish the sentence knowing what Nico would say next.

"I never noticed you had a birthmark on the back of your neck," Aaliyah said feeling left out.

"It's not really noticeable unless you're really paying attention," Nico said realizing his daughter wasn't taking this the way he had hoped. "Aaliyah, please know that no one will ever be able to take your place. Because Angel has come into our lives doesn't change my love for you. I have enough love to give to both of my beautiful daughters," Nico said pulling Aaliyah close for a hug.

"I hear you, Daddy."

"Good because as soon as I get out of this hospital I want the three of us to go out for dinner. It's time my favorite girls get to know each other." Nico beamed.

There was no denying how ecstatic Nico was to share his new found daughter to Precious, Aaliyah, and everyone else in his circle. For Nico, although Angel was a grown woman, he felt he was getting a second chance at fatherhood and he was going to cherish every moment.

Chapter Twelve

Perfect Puppet

When Justina told Aaliyah she had her own business to attend to while in Miami she wasn't lying. When Justina murdered Markell she not only tied up any loose ends to her working with Maya, but she also was about to score herself a huge payday.

"Hi, I'm Justina. I'm here to see Desmond." She gave a warm smile to the hostess who was more than happy to show her the way.

"I really love your shoes and purse. It matches perfectly with that outfit," the hostess complimented. The black crepe with thin white lines bra top and matching wide leg silhouette, high-waist fit pants did look stunning on Justina. She set the overall look with a Gucci Dionysus Striped Bamboo top handle bag and Gucci multicolored leather high heel sandals with gold pointed studs up the back of the heel. The high fashion yet casual, sexy look was well thought out by Justina. It was meant to seduce on the low with a touch of class.

"Mr. Blackwell, Justina is here."

"Thank you, show her in."

"Desmond, hello." Justina smiled reaching out her hand.

"Thank you for coming by." Desmond took Justina's hand and shook it.

"Thank you for meeting with me."

"Are you kidding me... I would've been crazy not to. I'm sure you could've presented your offer to several other people and they would've gladly accepted," Desmond said.

"You're probably right, but Markell always spoke so highly of you and how you handled business."

"Markell was a good dude. I was shocked when I heard he was murdered. I'm assuming the cops don't have any suspects."

"Unfortunately they don't."

"It figures. I'm sure his death isn't a priority to them. But yeah, I liked Markell. One time when he came to Miami he actually showed me a picture of the two of you. I think you all had recently came back from Acapulco."

"Yes, that was an amazing trip."

"Don't take this the wrong way, but you're much more beautiful in person."

"Thank you. That's very sweet of you to say." Justina blushed.

"Only speaking the truth. But let's get back to business. So you have a substantial amount of product you want to get rid of?"

"Yes. Before he was murdered he had just purchased a large quantity of drugs. Although I would help Markell with some of his deals, I have no interest in continuing to run his drug business."

"That's understandable. Moving drugs isn't an easy task especially with the amount you have. I know I presented a number to you, to take the drugs off of your hands. Is the price acceptable?" Desmond wanted to know.

"I think it's pretty fair. Although it is some of the purest coke you can get your hands on."

"I can't deny that especially since I know

who Markell's supplier was. But I am taking it off your hands and you don't have to do any legwork. I'll have my people pick it up and transport it. All you have to do is sit back and collect the cash. A small fortune might I add."

"How long will it take you to get me the money?" Justina wasn't showing it, but she was anxious to get her hands on all that cash.

"Could you hold on for one minute, Justina. I need to take this call."

"Take your time," she said scoping his office.

"Dale, what up my main man?"

"Ain't shit up. I've been meaning to hit you up, but things been a little hectic for me."

"Well, you are engaged, 'bout to be a married man so you get a pass," Desmond joked.

"Appreciate the understanding."

"You should." Desmond laughed. "You can make it right if you let me plan your bachelor party. I wanna do it right here at the club. I'll only have my best girls working. Real upscale, some nice shit."

"I don't know man. You can get a lil' wild and my fiancé ain't gonna be feeling that shit."

"Tell Aaliyah she can come too. It's all good. I just wanna show my man a good time. What you say."

"A'ight. I'ma let you plan that shit, but don't go crazy," Dale forewarned.

"Man, I got you. But listen, I got someone in my office. She's been waiting patiently." Desmond winked at Justina. "When you coming by so we can discuss business."

"I'll be there later on today. I'll call you when I'm on the way."

"Cool, see you later on, man. Sorry about that," Desmond said after hanging up. "That's one of my partners right there. We've been friends for years."

"How nice. I couldn't help but hear you mention a bachelor party. Sounds like fun."

"Yeah, my man is getting married soon. I have to send him off right."

"I'm sure you will." Justina giggled as the wheels began spinning in her head. She thought she had finally come up with the perfect way for Dale to learn the truth about his precious Aaliyah.

Clarissa had arrived at the club early and was about to get ready when she noticed an altercation going on between the new girl and Nesa. At first she was going to stay out of it and tried to ignore the bickering, but they was getting louder and louder. Then when Clarissa saw Nesa yank Dominique's wig off, she knew it was time for an intervention.

"You all need to chill!" Clarissa said calmly.

"You stay the hell outta this!" Nesa snapped. Clarissa looked at her dumbfounded.

"Excuse me!"

"You heard what I said. I'm 'bout to handle this bitch!" Nesa barked pointing the wig she yanked off Dominique's head in her face.

"Give me back my wig," Dominique screamed reaching for it, but Nesa wasn't giving up shit.

"Nesa, why you playin' wit' that girl like that?"

"Because this bitch done stole my best client. I'm 'bout to wipe the floor wit' her ass!"

"I ain't stole shit from you. It ain't my fault that nigga asked for me. I'm just doing my motherfuckin' job!" Dominique exclaimed.

"See if he'll be askin' for you after I break yo' face!" Nesa howled, lunging her claws at Dominique. Right before her nails made contact with Dominique's eye, Clarissa managed to yank Nesa's arm.

"That's enough! I ain't about to let you fuck

this girl's face up over no dumb shit," Clarissa roared. "Yo' ass gon' end up fired and in jail!"

Nesa was reeling in anger. She was huffing and puffing like she was ready to explode. She swung her arm loose from Clarissa's grasp and looked like she was ready to take both women down, but Nesa was smart enough to know she would come up short. Dominique was petite and easy to lay out, but Clarissa was tall, thick, and built. Nesa felt she might be able to hold her own with Clarissa, but wasn't willing to take that chance.

"I'm done here, but you better watch yo' back lil' mama. I knew yo' ass would be trouble when I saw you sashaying across that damn stage. But I done paid my dues and you ain't about to come up in here and take money out my motherfuckin' pocket. I got my eyes on you," Nesa spit in rage, pointing her two fingers at her own eyes and then turning and pointing the same fingers at Dominique.

Clarissa stood guard in front of Dominique until Nesa had walked off. "Don't pay her no mind," Clarissa said once Nesa was gone.

"Thank you so so much! I promise I thought she was gonna try and kill me," Dominique said picking her wig up off the floor. "I can't believe she came at me like that over a customer." Dominique was shaking, still nervous over the altercation.

"Girl, you in the big leagues now. That one customer is worth thousands and thousands of dollars to Nesa. These girls in here ain't playin'. Besides they basic needs being met, they got tits, lipo and ass surgeries to fund. They ain't tryna let no new girl walk up in here and take all they coins," Clarissa schooled her.

"So what am I supposed to do, not work here? Shit, I need the money too."

"I feel you. Just watch yo' back. Come in here, do your job, be cordial to these chicks and keep it moving. Everybody in her is out for self."

"If everybody is out for self, why did you help me?" Dominique asked.

"Because fair is fair. I don't like anybody coming at somebody else because they bigger and think they can easily whoop the other person. Especially when that person hasn't done anything to you. Nesa blow hard in your direction you might fall down... she know better." Clarissa shook her head.

"You right. I ain't gon' even lie, she had me scared. If you hadn't shown up, I'd probably still be trying to pick myself up off the floor right now." Dominique laughed and Clarissa joined in.

"Girl, you crazy! But I'm not going to let Nesa touch you or any other chick in here. I got yo' back."

"I don't know why you're being so nice to me, but thank you so much. Miami is way different then the small town I come from."

"I can only imagine. But we both need to get ready because if we don't hit that stage on time, Desmond gon' give all of us our walkin' papers."

From a short distance Justina had watched all the drama unfold. After her meeting with Desmond she managed to shake the hostess and do a little looking around. She was searching for the right person to help implement her plan and Justina was confident she had found the perfect puppet.

Chapter Thirteen

Motivation

"You have five more sets of pull ups to do. Don't get tired now!" Reggie barked at Darien like a drill sergeant.

"Man you killing me," Darien complained.

"Go 'head and quit then. You already lost yo' wife go 'head and lose your career too!" Reggie shouted getting Darien worked up.

"I ain't loss shit!" Darien roared, working out even harder. "Angel is still my wife and I will get her back." There was no denying Darien's determination as he finished his pull-ups and jumped straight into crunches using a band for resistance.

Reggie sat back and smiled. He had to keep Darien riled up in order to get the best out of him. That hunger in his eyes had finally shown back up. He knew Darien could rise back up to the top, but it would take more than willpower. It would take every ounce of strength he had. When they first got back in the gym, Darien wasn't fully committed. Reggie could tell that his protégé was mentally broken. The rift with his wife had him in a depressed state, but slowly he was stepping out from under the dark cloud that seemed to follow him.

Once Reggie decided to use the demise of his marriage to motivate Darien to step his game up, there had been a one eighty in how he trained. Darien was no longer fighting against his coach he was now battling himself and he wanted to win.

"Great workout today. The best so far," Reggie said patting Darien on the back of his shoulder. "At first I was skeptical. I wasn't sure if you wanted this, but today you proved that you do."

"I want Angel back. I want us to share the life we had talked about. She didn't fall in love with a weak man and if I have any chance of getting my wife back, I have to remind her that I'm the same man she vowed to spend the rest of her life with."

"Darien, I have no idea what's going to happen between you and your wife, neither do you. That's the thing, we don't have control over other people, but we do have control over ourselves. So when you're in that ring, remember you a champion. That's what you have to hold onto. Everything else will work itself out," Reggie stated convincingly.

Darien believed everything his coach was telling him, but it didn't deter him from his ultimate goal. He was going to get Angel back and there was nothing left to discuss.

Angel hadn't left her father's side once she got word that he was alert and anxious to see her. They spent hours together trying to make up for all the time they had been apart. This was the happiest Angel had ever been in her life. She felt a hole in her heart had finally been filled.

"Nico, there's something I've been wanting to talk to you about, but it's never seemed like the right time. Or maybe I'm just afraid," Angel admitted.

"You don't have to be afraid to tell me anything. I'm your father and I wish you would start calling me that instead of Nico."

Angel smiled before giving her father a warm embrace. "You are so amazing. When I imagined how my father would be, never in a million years did I think he would be as wonderful as you."

"I'm the lucky one."

"I doubt you'll feel that way when I tell you what I have to say."

"Whatever it is, we'll get through it together."

Angel sat across from Nico working up her nerves to come clean. She let out a deep sigh before speaking. "I'm the reason why you were shot."

"What do you mean?"

"Darien was shot on our wedding night in Hawaii. I found him bleeding to death. Before he was rushed to the hospital he told me that it was you that shot him. I was furious." Angel put her head down reliving that night.

"That's understandable. I would've been furious too."

"But if I had known you were my father, I would've never ever put that hit on you whether you were responsible or not."

Nico gave a slight smile. "That sort of loyalty is admirable."

"When I did find out you were my father, I did everything I could to stop it. That's the main reason I was desperately trying to track you down to warn you, but I was too late. I'm so so sorry. I hope one day you can forgive me."

"I already do. Darien is your husband and you were seeking retribution for what happened to him on your wedding night. I would've done the exact same thing. When you discovered the truth, you tried to make it right. It didn't go the way you hoped, but luckily I survived and here we are together. It all worked out." Nico took Angel's hand wanting her to know his forgiveness was real.

"I can't believe how understanding you're being. I don't deserve your forgiveness."

"Angel, stop being so hard on yourself. Gosh, if I beat myself up for all the mistakes I made, I wouldn't be able to sleep at night. Don't do this to yourself. Can I ask you a question?"

"Of course, anything."

"Is this why you and Darien are living apart right now?"

"Yes. He knew you were my father and never told me. He had no plans of telling me."

"How did Darien find out? I made sure that less than a handful of people knew."

"I have no idea. I was so furious I didn't even bother to ask him. The fact that he was willing to let me have my own father killed is unforgiveable."

"In fairness, I'm sure Darien honestly believed that I was responsible for the attempt on his life. If you wouldn't have placed the hit then he would have," Nico stated.

"If I knew you were my father then I wouldn't have allowed it. Plus, like I told Darien, you knew I was your daughter so you wouldn't have had him shot on my wedding night."

"I didn't even raise you, but you know me so well."

"I know that you're a good man. Unfortunately, I can't say the same thing about my husband."

"Angel, I'm no fan of Darien Blaze, but before I knew you were my daughter and I had you kidnapped, that man was willing to do anything to get you back. He does love you and in a way I can understand why he never told you that I was your father. I'm not excusing his behavior, but what I'm saying is, don't put me on a pedestal and knock him down because in a lot of ways we're one in the same."

"Are you saying I should take him back?" She

was surprised that Nico would even want her to consider that.

"I'm saying there is a reason you married him. There's a reason why the two of you fell in love. Only you know if you're willing to give that up, but he is your husband. That shouldn't be taken lightly."

"Nico... I mean Daddy," Angel quickly corrected herself.

"There you go!" Nico gave her a playful thumbs up.

"I'm getting used to it, but what I was about to ask you was, have you ever been married?"

"I have. I was married to Aaliyah's mother, but only briefly. We got an annulment a few months ago. But if I had my way we would still be husband and wife."

"She must be the woman I saw at the hospital."

"Yes, that's Precious."

"Why did you all get an annulment?"

"Because she's in love with another man, a man that she was married to for many years. It took me many years to accept it, but I have."

"I'm sorry. That must hurt."

"It does, but we share a beautiful daughter who is your sister. So I have no regrets and I don't want you to have any regrets either. If you still love your husband and think there's any chance of reconciliation, then you should at least try," Nico advised.

"Thank you for the fatherly advice. I think that's the best part of having you in my life. I have access to all your wisdom."

"Yes, you do and anything else I have is yours. You're my family, my daughter and I love you so very much."

"I love you, too."

"Good because I think it's time the two most important people in my life come together and share in my happiness." Angel stared at Nico like she was clueless to what he was alluding to. "I'm talking about you and Aaliyah. I want the three of us to have dinner together."

"I would love that!"

"You would?"

"Definitely! I can't wait to get to know my sister. Our initial introduction was shaky, but hopefully the second time will go a lot smoother." Angel beamed.

"I'm positive it will. Aaliyah can sometimes come off a bit harsh, but she's harmless. I think the two of you are going to end up being very close."

"Fingers crossed you're right." Angel smiled, excited about the idea of having a real family.

Chapter Fourteen

Second Chances

"Baby, we're getting married soon, but instead of being the happy bride to be, you've been moping around. What's up wit' that?" Dale asked, stroking Aaliyah's hair as they lay in bed.

"I am excited about our wedding, but finding out I have a sister has put me in such a funk." Aaliyah sighed.

"That's what's been bothering you?" Dale turned Aaliyah's face towards his. "You telling me you've been walking around with a frown on your face for the last few weeks because you found out you have a sister. Are you serious, Aaliyah?"

"Yes! All my father does is talk about Angel... Angel... Angel. He's even forcing me to sit down and have dinner with her. Like I need another sibling." Aaliyah rolled her eyes.

"I would do anything to have a sibling in my life."

"Dale, I'm so sorry. How insensitive of me. I know you're still having a hard time dealing with Emory's death."

"You mean his murder that no one has been held accountable for. I reached out to the detective who was working the case and he said it had been allocated to a cold case. It hasn't even been a year since he was killed. Them motherfuckers don't care about my brother, but I do. I'm not giving up so easily. Maybe they can't find his killer, but I damn sure will."

Aaliyah's body tensed up hearing Dale talk about finding his brother's killer. She thought that maybe some of his anger had subsided by now, but she could see that was only wishful thinking on her part.

"Baby, I hate seeing you in pain like this. At some point you have to let go. Like you said, we have an upcoming wedding. We're going to be husband and wife. This should be a positive time for us."

"Does that mean you gonna stop being angry about having a sister and instead get to know her?"

"I guess," Aaliyah reluctantly agreed, mainly because she wanted Dale to stop fixating on finding Emory's killer. If making nice with her newly discovered sister would make Dale back off, then so be it.

"I don't want an 'I guess'. I need to hear a strong yes," Dale pushed.

"Yes! Now are you satisfied?" Aaliyah punched Dale playfully in the arm.

"That means she'll be getting an invite to our wedding."

"Don't push it!"

"She's your sister, Aaliyah. If anyone deserves to be at our wedding it's her. Family is more important than anything. Don't ever forget that."

"You're right. I guess we'll be adding one more person to the guest list." Aaliyah gave Dale a fake smile and then decided to slide on top of him so they could have sex. She figured if they were too busy making love, it would keep Dale's mouth closed so he could stop talking about a sister she had zero interest in getting to know.

Aspen was minding her business getting ready for work when she saw that Clarissa was calling her. She damn near tripped over herself trying to answer her phone. "Girl, I hope you calling to tell me Rico is finally back in town," Aspen shouted.

"You ain't got to yell. I can hear you, but umm yeah I did call you about Rico. He's not back yet, but will be on Friday. He said he could meet up with us on Saturday. It needs to be early though cause I have to work a double shift. I'm in desperate need of some money," Clarissa said.

"Just tell me when and where. I'll be there. I need to find out what he knows."

"Don't get your hopes up too high because he might not know nothing more than what I already told you."

"True, but it won't hurt to try."

"No doubt. So I'll see you on Saturday. Thanks again, Clarissa. You always looking out for a sistah"

"No problem. You my girl, but I'll talk to you

before then. Gotta go. Bye!"

"Bye!" Aspen was ready to do the happy dance, but decided not to start celebrating just yet. She was happy that Rico's ass was finally back. This meeting was long overdue, but he had gotten a road gig doing security for some rapper so he had been MIA. Saturday couldn't get here fast enough as far as Aspen was concerned.

Aspen gave herself a once over in the full-length mirror one last time before grabbing her purse and heading out the door. She was doing a double date with Monique tonight and didn't want to be late. She was speeding, but not fast enough to draw attention from the police. When she arrived at the restaurant, Aspen glanced around the parking lot looking for Monique's car, but didn't see it.

"Let me find out I got here before Monique." Aspen smiled since she was known for being habitually late.

"Can I help you?" the hostess approached and asked.

"Yes, I'm supposed to be meeting my girlfriend here. We're having a double date. Her name is Monique, but I don't think she's here yet."

"Oh, you must be Aspen."

"Yes, I am."

"Monique isn't here, but another young lady is. I'll take you to her."

Aspen raised an eyebrow as she followed behind the hostess. She checked her phone to see if Monique had sent her a text, but there was nothing. They spoke yesterday morning when Monique confirmed everything so Aspen was perplexed that she was a no-show. Once the hostess took her to the table, Aspen thought she was going to choke.

"There you are!" Taren stood up and gave Aspen a hug.

"Taren! It's so good to see you although I'm a little surprised. Where's Monique?"

"Monique is a mess." Taren laughed as they sat down. "Last night she got a call to travel to Dubai and make some sweet money. Of course she couldn't pass up an opportunity like that. Thank goodness her passport was up to date," Taren joked.

"Really? I wonder why she didn't call me to let me know about the change of plans."

"Everything was so last minute. The only reason she had a chance to call me was because she needed me to cover her for the double date tonight. You know Angel and Desmond would've fired her ass if no one showed up for the date."

"So the Dubai trip wasn't through Angel's Girls?"

"Nope. A friend put her on to the trip. Lucky for her I was free tonight, so I was able to come in her place. Isn't this great! We haven't done a double date in forever." Taren smiled.

"Yeah, it's pretty awesome. So do you know who we're meeting tonight. Monique didn't really give me much info."

"They some business tycoons that come to Miami once or twice a month. I've done a double date with them before that's why I didn't have a problem stepping in because they cool. They're partners in a sports management company. Young and cute too," Taren added.

"So what time will they be here?"

"Soon, I'm sure. But you'll like them, they're a lot of fun and not one girl has ever complained. They also tip extremely well." Taren winked.

"Great!" Aspen was doing her best to disguise her revulsion for Taren. If she had any clue that she was going to show up in Monique's place, Aspen would've found a way to get out of the double date. Instead she was stuck with the one person she couldn't stand most in the world. Aspen wanted their dates to arrive ASAP. The sooner the night started, the quicker it would be over with.

"Angel, when I got your call I didn't know what to think. But I have to be honest, I was praying you wanted to tell me that you're coming home," Darien said.

"I'm not ready for that yet."

"Does that mean at some point you'll be open to a reconciliation? If I know you haven't completely closed the door on us then I have a reason to keep going."

"You look like you're doing great to me. I'm serious. You've come a long way in a short amount of time. I'm happy for you. As pissed off as I am with you, I still want you to be at your best."

"I'm at my best with you, Angel. You've been the driving force to getting back in the gym and training again. I never want you to see me as a weak man."

"Darien, it's not about that. When you were sick, I wanted to help you get better. Not because I thought you were weak, but because you were my husband."

"I still am your husband if only you would let me be."

"It's not that simple." Angel sighed, tugging at her ponytail.

"Baby, I know what I did was wrong. I made one of the worse mistakes of my life keeping the truth from you. I promise I will do everything in my power to make it right."

"You can start by telling me who told you I was Nico's daughter."

Darien put his head down for a second. He wasn't expecting Angel to ask him that, but he also had no plans of fucking up a chance to get back in good with his wife.

"Are you gonna tell me or not?"

"Nathan, one of the men that handles security for Nico. I don't know how he found out, but he gave up the information for a price. I paid a pretty penny for it too. The crazy part is at first I didn't want to believe it. It's no secret how I feel about Nico, but if it wasn't for him there would be no you."

"Darien, my father could've died."

"I know, but he didn't and don't forget I did almost die. I know you're adamant that Nico had nothing to do with it, but..."

"But what?"

"I can't help but feel like Nico knows who did try to kill me. But you know what, I don't even care about none of that shit. I just want my wife back. Baby, please give us another chance. You're my first love," Darien said gently taking Angel's hand.

"I can't make you any promises," Angel said pulling her hand away. "I'm still very much in love with you, but I'm having a hard time getting past the anger I feel towards you. I don't hate you, but there is a strong dislike."

"You have every right to feel that way. What I did was dead ass wrong. With time, I do believe you can get past the dislike. But that can only happen if you're open to it; willing to give us a chance. Have dinner with me tonight."

"Darien..." Angel shook her head.

"Please. You can pick the place and we can meet there. After dinner you go your way, I go mine."

"Fine, but only because you gave me that information about Nico."

"Whatever it takes," Darien said unbothered by what made Angel agree to have dinner with him as long as she did.

"But it can't be tonight. I have a meeting tonight, but tomorrow night would work."

"I'll take it. Thank you, Angel."

"Don't thank me yet. We're having dinner.

I'm not moving back in."

"At least you're willing to try. That's a start."

"I'll see you tomorrow night." Angel kissed her husband on the cheek and left, giving him the hope he desperately craved.

Chapter Fifteen

Emergency

Taren, Aspen, and their dates were partying the night away at Rockwell Nightclub. The spot was a combination of LA cool with New York music and Miami energy. They were all having a blast as the champagne kept flowing all night. The euphoric vibe was so contagious that for a minute Aspen put her guard down and forgot she hated Taren.

"This place is incredible!" Aspen yelled over the music to Taren. "We have to come back here again," Aspen continued, getting up from the booth and grinding her hips to the bass blaring from the state of the art sound system. Soon one of the men came up from behind and they danced with each other like they were in deep lust. Taren laughed with enthusiasm, thrilled Aspen was having a good time. She knew how those boys operated. The more fun you seemed to be having the more money flowed out their pockets.

Taren had got so caught up in watching Aspen's dirty dancing moves that at first she didn't see Aspen's phone ringing until it said missed call from Clarissa, a few seconds later a text message came through from the same person. Taren glanced up to make sure Aspen was still preoccupied. Then being the nosey heifer that Taren was, on the sly she picked up Aspen's phone to see what it said.

Rico just hit me. He'll be back in town tomorrow so he wants to meet Friday instead. Not sure if you're working that night, but it might be your only chance to grill him about Tony so make it work.

Taren put Aspen's phone down livid. *That sneaky bitch will not let sleeping dogs lie. She's trying to find out information about Tony, which can only mean she's investigating Laurie's murder.*

I really believed you had let that shit go, Aspen, but nope. If you keep this shit up, you'll leave me no choice but to get rid of yo' ass too, Taren surmised.

"Boss, It's good to see you back to your normal self. We were all rooting for you. But you Nico Carter, of course you was gon' be a'ight." Nathan chuckled taking a seat across from Nico in his office.

"I appreciate that, Nathan. If that shooter had been able to get off one more shot, I probably wouldn't be here talking to you right now."

"Nah, we wasn't gonna let that happen. We had yo' back like we always do."

"That's good to know because loyalty within my organization is essential. If you're not loyal, I have no use for you."

"Amen to that, boss. But your circle is tight and your team is strong so you don't have to worry about that from any of us," Nathan stated confidently.

"Do you like your job, Nathan?"

"Like it... I fuckin' love it!" He grinned widely.

"Interesting. So why would you fuck it all up by making an enemy of me?"

"Boss, is this some sort of joke?" Nathan laughed nervously. "Why would you say something like that?" he questioned, beginning to squirm in his chair and fidgeting his hands.

"Don't make shit worse for yourself by doing something stupid," Nico said, pulling out his heat and placing it on top of his desk with his finger resting on the trigger.

"Umm, Nico, I don't know what's going on wit' you, but you making a huge mistake. I ain't been nothing but loyal to you." Nathan sounded so sincere, but Nico knew he was full of shit.

"Is that why you sold my personal information to Darien Blaze's camp? You stupid, stupid, stupid boy." Nico shook his head with disdain. "I also know it was you that tried to kill Darien and make it appear that I was the one responsible. I'm also willing to guess that you were the one that killed Elijah since he was very much alive after that shootout at the hotel in Vegas."

Nathan bit down on his bottom lip knowing he had been caught. There was nothing he could say to talk his way out this shit so he did the first thing that came to mind which was to make a run for it.

"Sit yo' ass down!" one of Nico's security guards said, blocking the doorway. Then two more guards showed up surrounding the chair that Nathan was directed to sit back down in.

"Boss, it's not what you think."

"You can stop calling me boss because you don't work for me anymore," Nico scoffed.

"Whatever man. You gon' kill me anyway. No sense in me pretending that I like yo' mother-fuckin' ass," Nathan barked.

"Nigga, watch yo' mouth!" one of the guards barked, pistol-whipping Nathan. Nathan howled out in pain sounding like a wounded puppy.

"Chill," Nico said putting his hand up. "Let Nathan speak freely. Everyone in this room knows what's up. We don't have to pretend anymore, ain't that right, Nathan."

"Fuck you, Nico!" Nathan spat. The guard was about to go upside Nathan's head again, but Nico motioned for him to stop.

"Is there anything else you wanna tell me before I send you off to die?" Nico asked.

"Man, fuck you is what I wanna say. You ain't neva gave a fuck about nobody but yo' damn self. You didn't even flinch when Tony got killed. It was business as usual for you. You talk about loyalty, but you had all of us risking our lives so you could find yo' daughter. Like it was our mother-fuckin' fault you couldn't keep track of yo' kids. So go 'head and kill me, but just like I ain't like yo' ass and wasn't loyal to you, somebody in your precious daughter's organization don't like her ass neither. Now go choke on that shit."

Nico didn't bother letting his men handle his dirty work. Without even lifting up his gun, he pulled the trigger and sprayed four shots in Nathan's chest. "Get this scum out my office and clean this shit up," Nico ordered.

Taren cleared her entire day and night on Friday so she could stalk Aspen. She wanted to see who this Rico dude was and why Aspen thought he would have information regarding Tony. Taren trailed behind Aspen in a rental car she got for her excursion.

Aspen's first stop was a townhouse. When a tall curvy woman came out and got in the car, Taren figured that was Clarissa, the chick that had sent the text. Aspen had a tendency to drive fast so Taren was doing her best to keep up without being detected. Around fifteen minutes later the women pulled up to a rim shop.

"I know these bitches ain't shopping for rims," Taren huffed. "Ain't nobody got time for that and I mean that shit literally," Taren huffed some more, ogling the clock in her car. But after twenty minutes passed, Taren began to wonder if they were actually in there meeting with that Rico dude.

Taren debated what she should do. She really needed to see Rico's face in order to determine if he could reveal some shit to Aspen that would cause her problems. Taren decided if the women didn't come out in the next ten minutes she would have to walk her ass right over to that store and try to sneak a peek at the man.

Aspen was making Taren's head hurt by having her out there playing detective. "Fuck this bullshit!" she hissed getting out the car. She was about to slam the door when she saw Aspen and Clarissa coming out. Taren got back in her car and ducked down to make sure they didn't see her. She lifted her head up right above the steering wheel and that's when she noticed a man coming out right behind them. The three of them stood in front of the store and continued talking for a few more minutes.

"Fuck! Fuck! Fuck! I know that nigga! We

smoked together a few times." Taren wobbled her head erratically. "I don't think he know my name though because I definitely didn't remember his. Maybe he wasn't able to tell them shit." Taren was steady trying to reason with herself, wanting all this to go away. While Taren was arguing with herself she was interrupted by a call. "Hello!" she answered frantically.

"Hey, Taren. Is everything okay? You sound upset," Angel asked.

"Oh, I'm good. I'm driving and a police car was behind me with his siren on. I thought he was about to pull me over for speeding." Taren came up with a quick lie before Angel got suspicious.

"Well slow down. I'm sure you don't want a ticket."

"You got that right! So what's up?"

"I know this is last minute, but we're having an emergency meeting tonight. I'm calling every-one personally to let you know it's mandatory that you attend the meeting. I'll be sending out a group text with all the details."

"So what's this meeting about?" Taren was fetching for info, but Angel wasn't giving it up.

"I'll disclose all that information at the meeting tonight. See you there, bye!"

"I don't need this shit tonight," Taren muttered putting her attention back on Aspen. She was wrapping up her conversation with Rico and Taren would've given up her first born to hear what they were saying to each other. *Aspen, for your sake you better hope that nigga Rico didn't tell you shit, or else you'll be meeting the same demise as your girl Laurie*, Taren thought as she drove off.

Chapter Sixteen

House Of Lies

"Aaliyah, it's so good to see you," Nico said when she arrived at his house.

"I'm sorry I haven't been to visit the last few days, but this wedding planner I'm working with is totally anal."

"So why use her?"

"Because she's the best. That anal trait she has makes her super efficient. That means my wedding should go off without a hitch," Aaliyah said confidently.

"Well, I'm glad things are working out the way you want. My baby girl deserves the perfect wedding."

"I'm glad you said that because not only did I come by to check on you, but I also wanted to speak with you about something really important."

"Do I need to sit down for this?"

"Probably so."

"Then let me pour myself a drink while you talk."

"There's no easy way to say this so I'll spit it out. I want both you and Supreme to walk me down the aisle."

"I think I'ma need another drink," Nico said tossing one down and immediately pouring another.

"Please do this for me. Supreme has already agreed."

"Of course he did." Nico shook his head. "Supreme always has to be the level-headed good guy which I have no desire to be. I'm your father and it should be me that walks you down the aisle."

"Supreme is my dad, too. I know you hate

hearing that, but it's true. I lived in the same house with him practically my entire life."

"Humph, blame your mother for that."

"I feel blessed. I have two amazing men that I call dad. Not many people can say that. You said I deserve the perfect wedding. Do you want to be the reason that it's not?"

"You're really trying to pull at the heart strings. Fine, Aaliyah. I'll walk you down the aisle with Supreme," Nico conceded.

"Thank you, Daddy!" Aaliyah ran over to Nico and gave him a jubilant hug and kiss. "You're the best Dad ever."

"I'm sure you tell Supreme the same thing."

"What am I going to do with you, Daddy." Aaliyah laughed.

"You're going to return the good deed." Now it was Aaliyah's turn to be stumped.

"What good deed would that be?"

"Having dinner with me and Angel tomorrow night."

"I can't. I already have plans."

"Cancel them. I want you at dinner tomorrow."

"Why are you and Dale so pressed for me to connect with... with... with my," Alaliyah couldn't even say the word.

"Sister. You need to start practicing saying that. But to answer your question, the reason why we're so pressed as you worded it, is because Angel is your family. Family is more important than anything in this world."

Aaliyah turned away before locking eyes with her father. "What you're saying right now sounds so much like Dale. It's kinda scary."

"Why is that scary? It's good to know you're marrying a man that understands the importance of unity and loyalty within a family."

"How do you think my future husband would feel if he knew a member of my family is the reason he lost his? Answer me that because I know you are well aware that it was Supreme that killed his brother Emory."

"Of course I knew. Supreme told all of us when we were looking for you and your mother. It's no secret I loathe Supreme, but he did the right thing killing Emory."

"I doubt Dale would see it that way."

"Baby girl, unless you want to tell your fiancé the truth and deal with whatever ramifications comes with that, you need to let it go."

"I'm trying!" Aaliyah wailed. "But it's almost impossible to do when you and Dale are constantly throwing in my face the importance of family and loyalty."

"Working towards building a relationship with a sister you never knew you had is a hell of a lot different than revealing information about your fiancé's brother who was killed out of love for you. Don't compare the two," Nico made clear.

"You're right. I have to put Emory's death behind me. Dale knowing the truth would do absolutely nothing to strengthen our relationship; it would probably tear us apart. Keeping Dale in the dark is not only for my benefit, but his too."

"I agree. Some secrets are best kept buried."

With Nico's profound words, Aaliyah decided from this day forward she would never discuss the murder of Emory again.

"Good evening, ladies. I'm happy that each of you was able to make the emergency meeting. Although it was mandatory, so I guess I didn't leave you much of a choice," Angel simpered. "We all have things to do," Angel glanced over at Desmond, who was the one that demanded this little get together, "so let's get right to it."

"I'm aware that the police has recently been

questioning several of you about Laurie's death," Desmond stepped forward and said as if he was now taking over the meeting.

The women began looking around at each other as if trying to figure who had been questioned and who hadn't. Taren's attention immediately zoomed in Aspen's direction, but she didn't return Taren's glare. Aspen kept her focus on Angel and Desmond.

"Moving forward, if any police officer questions you, tell them to contact your attorney. Before you leave, each of you will be given the business card of the law firm we have on retainer to represent Angel's Girls," Desmond stated. "If I find out that any of you are cooperating with the police, your services will be terminated immediately."

All the women's eyes widened in disbelief and fear. Each of them wanted and needed their job, but they also didn't want any problems with the police.

"Ladies, I want to make something clear," Angel quickly interjected. "Just because we don't want you talking to the police without legal counsel that doesn't mean we're not committed to finding the person who is responsible for Laurie's murder." Angel put her attention back on Desmond wanting him to cosign on what she said.

"Angel is correct. We are working diligently to get justice for Laurie and we expect all of you to cooperate to help make that happen," Desmond said.

"Yes, so if any of you have information about what might have happened with Laurie, you need to come to us ASAP!" Angel made clear.

"Again, come to us NOT the police," Desmond stressed. "As Angel said when we first began, we all have things to do. So if no one has any questions we can wrap this meeting up."

"Actually I have a question," Aspen spoke up and said, raising her hand.

"What is it, Aspen?"

"You all said you're working on finding Laurie's killer."

"That's correct." Angel nodded.

"Have you gotten any leads?"

"Nothing concrete yet, but I promise you, we will find Laurie's killer. Laurie not only worked for Angel's Girls, but I considered her a friend so she will get justice." Angel was adamant.

"I can attest to that promise," Desmond said. "Adding on to what Angel said, having one of our girls murdered is bad for business. The longer it takes cops to find the killer, the longer they'll be harassing you all. So our number one priority is getting this cased solved."

Taren was in her chair freaking out and when she saw Aspen go over and start talking to Angel she was about to have a nervous breakdown on the spot. *What the fuck is that bitch telling Angel. Maybe that nigga Rico does know my name and spilled what he knows to Aspen and she's telling Angel right now. I have to get the fuck outta here! Don't move, stay right here Taren so you can see what happens because if Aspen don't know shit and I run then I'll look so fuckin' suspicious,* Taren had a full conversation going on in her head. Paranoia had her ready to jump out the window. She was beginning to think everyone in the room was staring at her like they knew she was guilty.

"Why are you still sitting here? The meeting is over," Meagan said, shaking Taren out of her thoughts. She looked around and saw that everyone was gone including Aspen and Angel.

"I was just thinking about how much I miss Laurie and got lost in my thoughts," Taren said.

"I know what you mean. We all miss Laurie, but I believe Angel will find her killer. I know it's hard, but try not to worry, it will all work out." Megan smiled.

Taren smiled back and got the fuck outta there. She had her own plans to make because Angel discovering the truth was not an option.

Chapter Seventeen

On Happy Family

Aaliyah and Nico were already seated at the swanky restaurant when Angel finally arrived. Being that mostly everything was a competition for Aaliyah, she was extremely annoyed that Angel got there after her. She wanted to be the one to make an entrance.

"What in the hell is she wearing!" Aaliyah balked, completely mortified. Both women had on the exact same burgundy dress with the mock neck, open shoulder, and keyhole back with ruffle detail. The only difference was the shoe selection. Aaliyah chose a simple nude heel whereas Angel decided to stand out from the rest by adding an umph to her look. She took the simple yet very pretty dress and paired it with some prune colored wild Russian suede/mink heels. The glamorous mink detail was at the top of the foot and at the end of the ankle tie. Angel literally dazzled from head to toe.

"Calm down, Aaliyah. I got the same dress for both of my daughters. I had no idea you would each decide to wear it tonight. I guess sisters do think alike." Nico smiled before standing up and hugging Angel before she sat down.

"Hi Aaliyah, it's such a pleasure to meet you."

"We already met... remember at the hospital," Aaliyah hissed.

"Yes, but that wasn't a proper introduction. I apologize; I could've been more welcoming. I was a little overwhelmed at the time."

"No need to apologize, Angel. Those circumstances were very difficult. Aaliyah understands... don't you, Aaliyah?" From the side of her eye, Aaliyah could see the disapproving stare her father was ready to give her so she played nice.

"Of course I understand. I could've handled things better myself. So I also want to apologize."

"That's my girl." Nico leaned over and kissed Aaliyah on the cheek. She looked over and gave her father that daddy's girl smile. "By the way, I love your dress, Angel."

"I love your dress, too." She giggled. "Our father has great taste right."

Aaliyah wanted to cringe. Hearing Angel call Nico father was like a stab in the heart. For all these years, she was the only one that had the right to say that word to him and that's how Aaliyah liked it.

"Are you okay?" Nico asked with concern because all of a sudden Aaliyah had become dead silent.

"I'm sorry, Daddy, I just remembered I was supposed to drop something off to the wedding planner and I forgot."

"I'm sure it can wait until tomorrow," Nico said ready for the waitress to take their orders.

"Wow, Aaliyah, you're getting married. Congratulations! I'm sure the wedding is going to be beautiful." Angel beamed.

"Angel, you'll be able to see for yourself. You'll be at the wedding," Nico chimed in and said to Aaliyah's dismay.

"Yes, I have to invite my sister. That would just be mean girl like if I didn't," Aaliyah said through clenched teeth.

"I would understand if you didn't want me to be there."

"Don't be silly, Angel. Of course Aaliyah wants you there. Don't you, Aaliyah?"

"Of course, Daddy. My father told me that you're actually married to the boxer Darien Blaze."

"Yes, I am."

"How long have you all been married? I heard he used to be a major playboy. I personally don't know any of the women he dated, but I used to see him in the blogs all the time with models, actresses, thots. You know the typical type of women that athletes date," Aaliyah said smugly.

"I own a dating service so I know exactly what type of women most athletes date and yes Darien used to be one of those guys. I was reluctant to date him for that very reason, but we fell in love and the rest is history. Hopefully, I made the right decision, but only time will tell."

"That's right baby girl," Nico said squeezing Angel's hand. "Darien is your husband and it's important that you give your marriage a chance."

"Your advice helped a lot."

"Darien is cheating on you already?" Aaliyah threw the accusation out there like she had first hand knowledge of what was going on in their marriage.

"No, nothing like that. We are dealing with a setback in our marriage, but it has nothing to do with infidelity," Angel said politely.

"Remember, both of you," Nico said looking at Aaliyah and Angel. "Because soon you'll be a married woman too, Aaliyah. All marriages go through setbacks, but it's about the get back. If you thought enough of the person to marry them, then you owe it to yourself to do everything you can to make the marriage work. Don't ever check out until you've given it your best and then some."

Angel and Aaliyah both nodded their heads in agreement with their dad. Aaliyah wasn't used to sharing her father, but she could tell he really loved Angel. He looked at Angel the same way Aaliyah was used to him looking at her which caused an undeniable jealousy. On the flipside, because of the genuine love Aaliyah saw that Nico had for Angel, it made her want to try harder to have a relationship with her sister.

"Where in the world is my driver's license!" Aspen yelled out, tossing everything out of her purse. She searched through her wallet for the third time before digging around her other purses. She started thinking about the last time she used her license and remembered last night when she and Clarissa went out for drinks she showed it to the bartender when he had ID'ed her. "Fuck! Did I leave it at the bar?" she questioned out loud.

Aspen called the hotel bar where her and Clarissa had drinks, when they didn't have it she decided to check with Clarissa.

"Hey girl, what's up?" Clarissa answered.

"Please tell me I left my driver's license in your car because I can't find it anywhere."

"Did you check the bar we went to?"

"Yep and they don't have it. I'm about to tear my apartment up looking for it."

"Hold on let me go back to my car and check," Clarissa said walking towards the parking lot. Aspen could hear the car door open and she was keeping her fingers crossed that it was in there. "I don't see it," Clarissa said, still looking.

"Dammit!" Aspen yelled, ready to pull her hair out.

"Girl, you better be happy I looked on the side of the seat."

"You found it?!" Aspen asked getting excited.

"Yep."

"It must've fallen out my purse when I was in your car. Can you please do me a huge favor? I'm running late for a client I have to meet. Can you please, please drop the license off to me?" Aspen begged.

"I would, but I just pulled up to work and you know Desmond don't play."

"Exactly, so I can't be late either. I'm meeting the dude at a hotel. He's a regular customer and he likes for me to already be there and butt naked when he arrives. He leaves my name at the front desk, but I have to show my ID before they'll give me the room key."

"Can't you stop here and pick it up?"

"Girl, from where the hotel is, it will take me all out the way. I'll be super late and he's so anal when it comes to time. Trust he'll call and report me. He's done it to another girl before. I would take my chances if Angel was the one still running the day to day operation, but Desmond..." Aspen sighed.

"Chile, I already know. That nigga so militant with it," Clarissa cosigned. "Wait! I might have a solution," Clarissa said noticing Dominique coming out the club. "Give me one second. I'll call you right back." Clarissa hung up with Aspen and ran towards Dominique before she got in her car.

"Hey, Clarissa! Is everything alright? You was running towards me mighty fast," Dominique commented.

"Are you getting off right now?"

"Yeah, I just finished up my shift. Why?"

"Remember you said you owed me for shutting down that Nesa situation," Clarissa reminded her.

"Of course I remember. What you need?"

"Can you please drop off this driver's license at my girlfriend's apartment? She needs it for work and doesn't have time to drive all the way over here to get it," Clarissa explained.

"Is that all! Girl, please, I still owe you 'cause that ain't no major favor." Dominique laughed.

"Thank you, girl! Here you go." Clarissa handed the license to Dominique. "The address on the license is where she currently lives. I'ma call her now and let her know you on the way. Thanks again!"

"No problem. She actually don't live that far from me," Dominique said glancing down at the street address. "I'll talk to you later," she said getting in her car and driving off.

After Clarissa placed a call to Aspen letting her know all was good, she went into work relieved it all worked out.

When Dominique pulled up to Aspen's apartment complex she had two things on her mind: Giving her the driver's license and using the restroom. She'd been holding it since leaving the club and felt her bladder was one second from exploding.

Knock... knock... knock

"Hey! You must be Dominique." Aspen was grinning hard when she opened the door. "Come on in."

"Thanks so much for inviting me in."

"Definitely! I'm about to offer you a drink and something to eat for bringing this over to me." Both women burst out laughing. "You have no idea how bad I needed it."

"It was no problem. Plus Clarissa really looks out for me at work so whatever she needs, I'll always have her back."

"Yeah, Clarissa good people. I've known her

so many years. That's my heart right there. She always come through for me. But umm I was serious about that drink. Can I get you something?"

"That would be great, but can I please use your bathroom first. I don't think I can hold it any longer." Dominique giggled nervously.

"Of course. It's straight down the end of the hall."

"Thanks!" Dominique rushed to the bathroom and Aspen was headed to the kitchen to pour her drink when she heard a knock at the door.

"I wonder who that is," Aspen said opening the door not even bothering to look through the peephole.

"Hey Aspen! I'm so glad you're home." Taren had a cheerful expression as she basically bombarded her way through the door.

"Taren, what are you doing here?" The shock of opening her door and finding Taren's ass standing there had thrown Aspen off. That was the only reason Taren was able to slither her way in.

"I was in the area and since we can never seem to find the time to go out for that drink, I decided to bring the drink to you," Taren said pulling out a bottle of pink Moscato.

"This really isn't a good time for me, Taren. I have to get ready for work."

"You never seem to have time for me anymore, Aspen. It's always one excuse after another. I thought we were friends." Taren had a haunting tone in her voice.

"I think you need to go. Like I said, I have to get ready for work."

"I don't like your attitude, Aspen."

"Well, bitch, I don't give a fuck. I don't like you, now get the hell out of my apartment!" Aspen snapped, unable to contain her contempt for Taren any longer.

"So all that talk about putting Laurie's death behind us and being friends was bullshit, Aspen? You've really hurt my feelings."

"Taren, you have no feelings. I know you had something to do with Laurie's death and I'm this close to proving it." She pointed her finger assertively.

"Let me guess, you think that Rico dude is going to give you the proof you need?" Taren smirked.

"How the fuck you know about, Rico? You know what it doesn't even matter," Aspen yelled. "Yo' ass is going down and I'm going to be right there, front and center, cheering as they carry you off to jail. Now get the fuck out my apartment before I whoop yo' trifling ass!" Aspen barked, storming towards the door to throw Taren out.

"I told you to leave it alone and not fuck wit' me, but you had to get your Nancy Drew on. Big fuckin' mistake," Taren spit.

Aspen didn't even have an opportunity to react. In that brief second of having her back turned to open the door, Taren reached in her purse, got her gun, and busted off two bullets. One hit Aspen in the back, the other right through her head, causing brain matter to splatter across the door. Taren grabbed her Moscato bottle, pulled out a glove from her purse to open the door and stepped over Aspen's dead body like she was some trash in the street before exiting out.

Dominique remained locked in the bathroom scared to death. She had left her purse in the car so she couldn't even get her cell phone and dial 911. Her anxiety ran so deep, not knowing if the shooter would come back or even worse, if she was still in the apartment looking around to see if anyone else was there. Dominique's terror left her body so paralyzed in fear, there was a chance she would stay in that bathroom forever.

Chapter Eighteen

Paranoid

"Justina, I know we've been going back and forth with pricing, but I'm glad we've finally come up with a deal that we both feel is mutually beneficial," Desmond said shaking her hand.

"I hope I didn't offend you, but wanted to make sure I got the best deal possible being this was a one time shot."

"No doubt. That's how business should be done. If you didn't weigh all of your options, that's a clear indication you don't have a clue what you're doing. I respect the fact you know what you have is valuable."

"Thank you, Mr. Blackwell." Justina gave Desmond a subtle flirtatious smile.

"So are you rushing back to New York immediately after you receive all this money?"

"No. I like Miami. I thought I would stick around a little while longer. See what else the city has to offer."

"Glad to hear that."

"Why is that?" Justina questioned.

"A friend of mine is getting married."

"That's right. I think the first time I came to your office you spoke to him about doing his bachelor party."

"Yes, that friend. He doesn't want a bachelor party. Personally I think he's worried about what his fiancé would think." Desmond laughed. "I respect that he doesn't want to cause any drama before they even have a chance to say 'I do.'"

"Sounds like a smart man."

"Yeah, Dale is a pretty smart guy. But umm, since he doesn't want to have a bachelor party he's agreed to let me throw him an engagement pre-wedding party."

"Sounds interesting."

"I'm always looking for an excuse to have a blow out at the club. They've been engaged for a minute so this isn't technically an engagement party and they're wedding is around the corner, but still a few weeks off. I guess this is the in-between-stage party... if that's such a thing."

"If it's not, I'm sure you will make it."

"That's the plan. I'm going all out. This is a strip club so it won't be the traditional type party, but it will be a lot of fun. Of course all the big names that are in Miami will come out, but I want the major celebrities flying in from all over too. Super upscale with a touch of risqué, like my strip club."

"Sounds like it will be amazing," Justina said.

"Glad you think so because I would like for you to be my guest."

"Really?!"

"Yes, I hope that won't be a problem. Not sure if you've already started dating again. I can't imagine a beautiful woman like you being single for long."

"I am seeing someone that I've known since childhood. He's been really supportive while I've been dealing with Markell's death."

"I'm sure he has." Desmond gave a sly grin.

"He has a lot of business he needs to handle

in New York, so I don't think he'll be able to attend your party, but I would love to come."

"Wonderful, then it's a date."

"Let's not call it a date," Justina said playing coy. "How about your friend."

"Whatever you say as long as you're here."

"I will be."

"It's a black tie affair so come looking like a superstar which won't be hard at all for you since that's your everyday style."

"Desmond, you are really laying it on thick and I love it!" Justina giggled. "But I need to be going. I have a shopping date with my one of my girlfriends."

"Maybe you can pick something out for the party. It's next Friday. I can have my driver pick you up."

"I'll let you know." Justina waved bye to Desmond and left his office feeling a twinge of excitement for a few reasons. She initially thought when she contacted Desmond he would be the perfect person to put a small fortune in her bank account. Justina had no idea he would be so damn fine which was a bonus. On top of that he was cool with Aaliyah's fiancé Dale, so he was serving all sorts of beneficial purposes. If Justina didn't have plans to bring down not only Aaliyah but Amir too, she would seriously consider dating Desmond, but then again plans are meant to be broken.

Angel and Darien held hands as they strolled along the beach. The cerulean water, pale sand and vast open sky made for the most romantic backdrop imaginable.

"Dinner was incredible the other night. I'm not talking about the food either although that was exceptional," Darien said as he watched Angel's hair blowing from the early evening breeze.

"I can't lie it was nice. Can you believe that was the first time we'd been out for dinner since getting married?"

"I know. Things have been nothing short of crazy since our wedding day and I think the romance is what's been missing."

"Between you getting shot then my father getting shot, there hasn't been much time for romance."

"Maybe our dinner the other night will change that. I think we needed to hit the reset button. Give ourselves a fresh start. I really want you to move back home, Angel."

"I don't know if I'm ready for that, Darien," Angel confessed.

"You keep saying that, but how are we supposed to get back on track if you're living at a hotel? You're my wife. We need to be together under the same roof if this marriage has a chance."

"You're right, but I'm having a hard time forgiving you for what you did to my father."

"I get that, but Nico is straight now. You even said yourself that he told you to work on our marriage."

"He did, but..."

"Listen, I wasn't sure how you would take this, but I called Nico," Darien said cutting Angel off.

"You did... why?" she asked shocked by what Darien said.

"To apologize."

"But you hate my father."

"But I love you and I'm trying to make things right. It was only a phone call, but it's a step towards forgiveness. Surprisingly, Nico was very forgiving. He really loves you, Angel. Much more than he hates me. That's why he was able to forgive me."

"I appreciate you calling him. I know that had to be hard for you."

"I'll humble myself and call Nico everyday if that means you'll come back home."

"You're so silly." Angel laughed.

"But I'm so serious. I miss you. I bought that house for you. That entire home was decorated with you in mind. Everywhere I turn I'm reminded of you. I don't want to be there if you're not with me."

Darien stopped mid-step and held Angel closely as the water rippled across their bare feet. The warm sand seemed to be melting around them. "You're the love of my life, my soul mate. I want to share my life with you. Every day I've been in that gym, training to get back on top, it was you that motivated me. When I wake up in the morning, it's your face I want to see lying next to me in bed. Baby, please come home."

"Okay, I'll come home."

Darien lifted up Angel's face so he could search the inside of her soul through her eyes. "You mean that?"

"Yes, I'll come home. You're the first and only man I've ever been in love with. I want to share my world with you too, but Darien, don't ever keep secrets from me again. Without trust we have nothing."

"I promise that will never happen again. I'm going to spend the rest of my life making you the happiest woman in the world. I love you, babe."

"I love you, too."

For a second Angel and Darien stopped time as their lips locked and they remembered all the reasons they fell in love.

It was the middle of the night when Taren woke up in a cold sweat having nightmares about Aspen's death. She kept going over the sequence of what happened making sure she had covered her tracks. It was at that moment Taren realized the glove she used to open and close Aspen's door was gone. *It must've dropped when I was leaving,* Taren thought as her paranoia was on ten.

Taren threw on some leggings, a tank top, flip-flops and grabbed her purse then rushed out her apartment headed back to Aspen's place. Taren was making deals with the devil the entire ride over that Aspen's body hadn't been discovered yet. She turned off her headlights once inside the apartment complex. She wanted to draw as little attention to herself as possible.

From the parking lot it looked dark in Aspen's apartment. She didn't see any police on the scene or no crime scene tape, so Taren was optimistic the devil still had her back. With caution, she headed towards Aspen's apartment. Once she got there she quietly turned the doorknob and it was still unlocked just how she left it. "Not to self, wipe down this doorknob too before I leave," Taren said.

It was pitch dark so Taren turned on the light switch so she could see. "There you are!" she said happy to find the glove she dropped right next to Aspen's dead body. A few feet away she also noticed a tube of her favorite lipstick that must've also fallen out her purse earlier. "Thank goodness I came back."

Now that Taren was back and saw she had made two potentially costly mistakes she decided to triple check everything. She was going through the apartment checking areas that she had been nowhere near. But her brain was on full alert so she had to check everything. She had on both gloves so Taren felt good knowing no fingerprints would be left behind.

"All this searching make me need to use the bathroom," Taren said walking towards the restroom she knew was at the end of the hall. "What the fuck," she mumbled when she couldn't get the door open. "This shit is locked, oh shit, that must mean somebody in this motherfucker!" Taren shrieked shaking the doorknob like a crazy person. She then ran to the living room where she left her purse and got her gun before rushing back to the bathroom. "Whoever is in there you better open this motherfuckin' door before I shoot it open.

A few seconds went by and still nothing. The door didn't open which pissed Taren off even more. "Oh you wanna play! Have it yo' mother-fuckin' way!" Taren yelled ready to cock her gun and shoot.

"Please! Please don't shoot me!" Dominique cried out after opening the door.

Chapter Nineteen

Bad Decisions

Clarissa was driving on her way to the nail salon for a mani and pedi when she noticed Rico was calling her. "Hey, what's up?" she said making a right at the light.

"I was calling to find up what's up wit' yo' homegirl. I've been waiting for thirty minutes now for her to come through. She was gonna show me some pics and shit of this Taren chick."

"That's not like Aspen not to show up. Maybe she's running late. Did you try calling her?"

"Yeah, I've been blowing her phone up but nothing. I have someplace to be soon so I can only wait for another fifteen minutes. I know she said this shit was important, but I gotta go."

"I understand. I'ma call her now. If she don't answer then I'll stop by her apartment. I'll hit you back once I find out what's going on," Clarissa said ending her call with Rico and immediately calling Aspen. "Why aren't you answering your phone." Clarissa shook her head becoming worried. She made an illegal U-turn and headed to Aspen's apartment.

Aspen had a tendency to always run late, but to not answer her phone was a no go. She carried her phone around like some women carry a baby on their hip...very close. The only time Aspen didn't answer a call was when she was working, but she had a special voicemail message that would come on. This was sending a chill down Clarissa's spine as she hurried to check on Aspen praying that she had overslept after a long night at work.

The first thing Clarissa noticed when she got to Aspen's apartment was that not only was her car in the parking lot, but so was Dominique's.

She dashed up the stairs and almost tripped. Her heart was racing because even though she was telling herself that everything would be okay, in her gut she knew her life would never be the same again. Clarissa knocked on Aspen's door and then something just told her it was unlocked. She put her hand on the doorknob and hesitated because Clarissa was scared at what she might discover behind the door.

"Dear God, no!" Clarissa wailed when she saw Aspen's dead body lying on the floor. Part of her face was missing from the bullet to her head. Clarissa bent down and cried her heart out. She then remembered seeing Dominique's car outside and started looking around the apartment expecting to find her dead too but there was nothing. It was as if Dominique had vanished.

Clarissa then called Dominique, but her phone went straight to voicemail. The next call Clarissa made was to the police.

Justina had been tracking Nesa's moves from the day she spotted her having that epic encounter with another stripper at the club. By this time she knew that every Wednesday morning Nesa went to the beauty salon to get her hair done. She either got a fresh weave or got her weave touched up but she kept her hair did.

This particular morning when Nesa walked out the salon, instead of being greeted by whistles from lusting males it was Justina who wanted her attention.

"Do I know you?" Nesa questioned when she saw the unfamiliar face waiting by her car.

"Not yet, but if you have lunch with me I promise to make it worth your time," Justina said.

"Girl, I don't even know you," Nesa popped like who the fuck is you.

Justina knew the language Nesa understood and responded to. She pulled out a few hundred dollars and put it in Nesa's hands. "This is just to talk."

"Show me the way," Nesa said happy to be starting her morning off with a payday.

Justina and Nesa went to a restaurant in the same strip mall as the beauty salon. Justina was well aware she was taking a risk bringing Nesa in the fold, but she'd done her research and had a feeling Nesa was the perfect messenger.

"Let me guess. You have a feeling your man is fucking around and you want to use me to set his ass up. I'll do it for five hundred," Nesa said ready for another serving of the fresh butter rolls.

"No, that's not it."

"Then what? Oh your boyfriend has a birthday coming up and you want to surprise him with a threesome. I can do that too, but it'll cost you a thousand. It will be his best birthday ever." Nesa winked.

"How about I just tell you what I want so you can stop guessing," Justina said tired of listening to Nesa give her theories.

"My bad... go ahead. You are the one that's paying."

"Thank you. So next Friday your boss is having a huge party at the strip club you work at."

"How you know about that?"

"Because I was invited."

"Excuse me," Nesa mocked. "I didn't mean to offend you."

"No offense taken. But before I tell you what I want you to do, would you be willing to relocate? I'm sure you'll be able to get a job at another strip club."

"You want me to leave Miami?"

"Yes. It would be in both of our best interest."

Nesa was frowning her face at Justina, trying

to figure out what the well-dressed, articulate woman wanted her to do. She appeared to be harmless, but looks can be deceiving.

"For the right price I'll relocate to anyplace you like," Nesa stated.

"That's all I needed to know. Now this is what I need for you to do..." Nesa listened intently as Justina laid out her plan.

"I told you, I don't know anything," Dominique said between sniffles. Taren had slapped her across the face so many times all she wanted to do was go home and forget what had transpired in the last forty-eight hours. After Taren dragged her out of the bathroom by gunpoint, she made Dominique get in the trunk of her car. She then brought her back to her apartment, tied her up, put tape on her mouth, put her in a closet and went to bed. Killing Aspen, then going back to her apartment to cover her tracks to then discover a potential witness had drained Taren of all her energy. Sleep was the only thing that would give her the reboot she needed.

"Do you want me to slap you across the face

again!" Taren barked. "Next time I won't use my hand, I'm going to beat you with my fist," she threatened.

"I swear, I don't know Aspen. When I went to her apartment to drop off her driver's license was the first time I had ever met her."

After a few hours of slapping Dominique around and still getting the same response, Taren was starting to believe the chick was telling the truth.

"So how did you end up with Aspen's driver's license?"

"I was doing a favor for a girl I work with."

"Where do you work?" Taren was curious to know.

"I work at a strip club."

"Which one?"

"Diamonds & Pearls."

"Damn! You work at the club Desmond own." Taren shook her head.

"You know Desmond?"

"Yes, he's my boss."

"I've never seen you at the club do you work at one of his other clubs?" Dominique asked.

"Not that it's any of your business, but he's a partner in an escort service I work for. I can't believe you work for him too."

"That won't be a problem. I told you if you let me go, I won't tell anyone what I know."

"I need you to shut up so I can figure out what to do!" Taren snapped. She then put tape back over Dominique's mouth and put her back in the closet before locking the door.

Taren poured herself a stiff drink and sat on her balcony trying to come up with a strategy. *I can't keep this chick stashed in my closet for too much longer, but I can't just kill her either. At this rate, if I keep dropping bodies the police gonna start thinking there's a serial killer on the loose,* Taren reasoned. *But I have to come up with something quickly before Desmond and Angel start to realize that all clues point in my direction. If only I could get rid of them all in one pop that would make my problems disappear instantly. There has to be a way and I will figure it out,* Taren promised herself before pouring another drink and lighting a blunt.

Chapter Twenty

Moment Of Clarity

"Mr. Blackwell would like to see you in his office," the hostess informed Clarissa when she arrived for work. "Follow me."

Clarissa dreaded every step she took, as she got closer to Desmond's office. The police had already interrogated her; she could only imagine the questions her boss was about to beat her over the head with. Desmond was on the phone when she entered his office and he motioned for her to have a seat, which she did. With the terse expression on his face and the derisive tone of his voice, Clarissa knew he wasn't in a very good mood.

"What the fuck were you thinking calling the police!" Clarissa hadn't realized Desmond was off the phone so at first she didn't know it was her he was shouting at. But when he followed it up with, "What... you can't hear? Answer my fuckin' question!" Clarissa knew she was the target of his rage.

"I guess you're talking about Aspen's murder?"

"What the fuck else would I be talking about?" Desmond scoffed.

"I found my best friend dead in her apartment. Who else was I supposed to call?"

"You should've called me. You're well aware that Aspen worked for Angel's Girls and I'm a partner in that company. Your first call should've been to me."

"I didn't realize you handled legal matters."

"Don't get smart with me. You need to watch your fuckin' mouth because I'm the last person you wanna have problems with," Desmond warned. Clarissa didn't scare easily, but the glare in his eyes had her shook. She was sharp enough to know that unless she wanted to be found in some back alley dead it was time to back down.

"My apologies. When I arrived at Aspen's apartment and saw she was dead and Dominique was nowhere to be found I was worried so I called the police. I'm sorry, you're right I should've called you first." The apology seemed to take Desmond's anger down a few notches. "So still no word on Dominique?"

"No. She's vanished without a trace. The cops don't know whether she's a victim or the shooter. I told them there's no way Dominique would ever hurt Aspen, but they don't have any leads." Clarissa wanted to fully cooperate with Desmond so he would get off her back.

"You said Aspen was your best friend."

"Yes, she is, I mean she was before she died," Clarissa said solemnly.

Desmond was now sitting on the edge of his desk with his hand resting over his thinly groomed mustache. His intense gaze had Clarissa feeling like she was experiencing early menopause with the hot flashes she succumbed to.

"Lets start from the beginning. I need you to tell me everything Aspen was up to and why someone would want her dead. And Clarissa, don't leave out a single detail."

Clarissa swallowed hard before spilling everything she knew about her now deceased best friend Aspen.

Taren was on her way to the gym for an intense workout. Whenever she was stressed or felt overwhelmed, exercising always seemed to give her a clear outlook. Never mind that she was the cause of her own problems, Taren only wanted to find a way out. Her head was spinning to the point that when she saw Monique calling she ignored it, but she kept calling back.

"What is it, Monique!" Taren snapped.

"Omigosh, did you hear about Aspen!" Monique screamed frantically.

"I've been sick so I haven't talked to anyone. What happened to Aspen?" Taren questioned as if she didn't already know.

"She's dead, Taren. Aspen is dead!"

Taren rolled her eyes because this was the main reason she didn't feel like taking Monique's call. She wasn't in the mood to pretend like she cared or gave a fuck about Aspen. Now she was forced to put on a fake production not to raise suspicion.

"What happened... what she in some sort of accident?" Taren mustered up her best I care voice.

"No! She was shot and killed. First Laurie now Aspen, who's next! I'm starting to think Angel's Girls is jinxed."

"So Aspen was murdered. Who would do such a thing?" Taren said looking at the clock on the dashboard of her car trying to come up with an excuse to get Monique off her phone.

"Hopefully the police will do their job and find this crazy psycho soon. I love the money I make and the guys I meet doing this job, but this is becoming too much. Then we have this party we have to attend next Friday. I really don't feel like going," Monique nagged.

"What party?" that was the first thing Monique said that sparked Taren's interest.

"You must not have checked your text messages."

"No, I told you I've been sick."

"Desmond is having this big party at his strip club next Friday and we're all supposed to go. Of course he made it seem that it was mandatory we attend. Honestly, at first I was looking forward to it. I'm sure there will be a ton of money to be made that night, but with everything that's been happening I might have to pass."

"Well you have to do what you have to do, Monique. If Angel's Girls isn't the place for you anymore, maybe you should quit," Taren suggested.

"I didn't say I wanted to quit, Taren." Monique gasped sounding frazzled. "All I'm saying is..."

"Monique, I have to go. That's Angel on the other line," Taren lied before ending the call. Although Angel wasn't calling that was Taren's next move.

Please... Please... Please answer, Taren begged while the phone was ringing.

"Taren, hi."

"Thank goodness you answered. Are you okay?" Taren asked in her best concerned voice.

"No, I'm not. I don't know what is going on. Laurie and Aspen... I'm starting to think someone is out to destroy me and my business. Why else would my girls keep getting targeted like this?" Angel sounded defeated. "If I can't protect you all, how can I continue to run Angel's Girls?"

"Angel, none of this is your fault. You're a victim too."

"Tell that to Laurie's and Aspen's families."

"I understand, but you have to be strong, Angel. The police will find the killer or killers. Until then we have to maintain a united front. I know Desmond is your partner, but you're still the face of Angel's Girls. You started that company and the girls that work there love you. You have to let them know you still committed to the business and them." Taren was laying it on heavy and of course it was for her own self-serving reasons.

"That's crazy you're saying all of this because I was really considering handing over the business to Desmond. I had even decided I wasn't attending this party he has coming up because I no longer wanted to be affiliated with anything that had to do with Angel's Girls," Angel divulged.

"You can't do that. There's no Angel's Girls without Angel. We need you."

"I'm so glad you called, Taren. I needed this. Angel's Girls is my baby and I'm not going to let some monster with a vendetta against me ruin what I built."

"Does that mean you'll be attending the party?"

"Yes, and I expect you and all the other girls to be there too! Thanks again for the pep talk, Taren. You're the best!"

"That's what friends are for."

"Very true and you've been my friend longer than anyone else. I know I've been distant lately and I'm sorry," Angel said. "Darien and I had some marital issues, but we're good now. I also discovered who my father is and that I have a sister."

"Wow, that's amazing, Angel."

"It is now, but when I was finding all this out I wasn't sure if I would get that happy ending."

"Well did you?"

"Yes! This is the happiest I've ever been. I have my husband, my father, and a sister. I have a real family now. My personal life is finally wonderful now I have to get my professional life in order."

"I'm sure you will. Things always seem to work out in your favor, Angel." Taren sounded sugary sweet, but there was nothing but malicious undertones in what she said. She never forgave Angel for knowing Gavin was the person who killed her father, but instead of telling her, she kept the secret to herself.

Now that Angel shared with Taren she had her own father back in her life, it sent her jealously and hatred into overdrive. Angel had a father, a husband and even a damn sister yet Taren felt she had nothing.

"Taren, are you there?!" Angel called out.

"Sorry about that. I accidentally dropped my phone. What were you saying?" Taren asked making up a quick lie.

"I said at the party I'll be able to introduce you to my sister Aaliyah. She's getting married and Desmond is a good friend of her fiancé. He's actually throwing the party in their honor."

"Awesome! This is perfect. It sounds like it's gonna be a night to remember. I can't wait!" Taren smiled, preparing to put her evil plan in motion.

"So this is where we're getting married," Dale stated looking at the images Aaliyah was showing him.

"Yes! Isn't this place amazing. It's an Italian Villa right on the water and complete with stunning formal gardens. It has more than a hundred years of Miami history and this is where we'll begin making our history as husband and wife." Aaliyah then turned to give Dale a passionate kiss and started to undress him.

"Baby, baby, you know how much I love being inside of you, but I'm already running late,"

Dale said as Aaliyah continued kissing him and he almost couldn't resist.

"They can wait," Aaliyah whispered, licking her tongue on Dale's earlobe.

"I've cancelled this meeting with Desmond twice already. The party he's throwing for us is in a few days. I really need to go. I'll make it up to you tonight," Dale promised, placing his own tongue and gently biting down on the curve of Aaliyah's neck.

"You know that's my hot spot," she purred.

"Sorry babe, I couldn't help myself." Dale laughed. "Let me stop before I get myself worked up. I'm sure Desmond will be calling soon telling me to hurry up."

"So this party is really happening?"

"I've been talking to you about this party for the last few weeks so I'm assuming that question was a joke."

Aaliyah let out a deep sigh. "Planning this wedding has been so time consuming. Let's just say I'm not looking forward to getting dressed up for a huge bash and schmoozing with a bunch of people I don't know."

"I thought you loved having a reason to get dressed up and show off," Dale teased putting his hands around Aaliyah's waist and pulling her close. "Also, I'll be there and didn't you say your sister is coming so you'll have familiar faces around you."

"My sister! Wow, I'm having a hard time hearing you say that out loud."

"I thought you said things went well at the dinner with your father and Angel."

"I guess. She's okay, but I don't need a sister. I have Justina for that. I've also known her way longer than Angel. We've had our problems, but she's been like a sister to me. Don't forget Justina also saved my life."

"Justina seems nice and I'm glad you have her. But never underestimate the importance of your blood family. They'll come through for you in ways that nobody else will. Embrace your sister. You never know, she might be the one that has your back when nobody else does. I'll see you when I get home."

Once Dale's words sunk in, Aaliyah knew he was right, but her jealously kept her from embracing Angel. She never wanted to admit it, but she loved having all of Nico's attention. For so long, Aaliyah was the only person besides Precious that Nico adored. Now she had to share that adoration with Angel and it was much more difficult than Aaliyah ever imagined.

Chapter Twenty-One

Man Of My Word

"A day of shopping was the perfect idea," Aaliyah commented as her and Justina browsed through the shops at Bal Harbour.

"I figured you would think that since it was your idea." Justina giggled. "But I'm down for it especially since we've planned and cancelled this outing like three times."

"I know, but I've been so busy lately. Who

knew planning a wedding could be this much work," Aaliyah said shaking her head.

"But you have a wedding planner. Isn't that what you hired her for?"

"True, but I have to stay on top of her. She's always coming up with her own ideas, but there are specific ways I want everything to be so I have to micro manage her ass. I want my vision to come together perfectly. I mean you only get married once, well at least that's what I'm hoping," Aaliyah snickered.

"I'm sure it will be flawless. The venue alone is fabulous. I mean the Vizcaya is breathtaking."

"It really is. I was thrilled it was available on the day I wanted. People reserve that place years in advance. Don't forget to come over for you final fitting. You are my maid of honor."

"I told you I'll be over this weekend."

"That's right. I have so much on my mind, I forgot. I'm still debating if I should ask Angel to be a bridesmaid. I know my father really wants me to."

"What do you want?"

"I want to pretend that I'm still my father's only daughter. Like I told Dale, I already have a sister... you!" Aaliyah beamed, blowing Justina an air kiss, which she returned.

"Then invite her to the wedding and that's it. Nico has to understand that relationships take time to build. You just found out she's your sister. If you all are meant to be close then it will happen."

"I agree. Dale and my dad are putting way too much pressure on me to have this instant sisterly bond with Angel."

"So how is she anyway?" Justina was curious to know. "Initially when you thought she was Nico's girlfriend you hated her guts, has that changed now that you know she's your sister?"

"Honestly, Angel's gorgeous, smart, and sweet which makes me hate her even more." They both laughed. "But seriously I do kinda like her. I was somewhat bitchy towards her at dinner, but she kept cool the entire time. If I were in a situation where I was under pressure, I would want Angel on my team. She has this icy calmness about her, kinda like my dad," Aaliyah said raising an eyebrow.

"Interesting. I can't wait to meet her."

"You will, if you come to this pre-wedding party if that's what you want to call it."

"I told you I'm coming. Besides, the guy Desmond personally invited me," Justina said holding up a long sleek silver dress that was calling her name.

"That's super sexy," Aaliyah remarked, mad she didn't see the dress first. "You did mention you knew the guy Desmond. How did you all meet anyway?"

"A mutual friend."

"I see. Does Amir know about your friendship with Desmond?" Aaliyah inquired.

"There's nothing to know. He's cool and he invited me to a party I would be attending anyway, so there's nothing to tell."

"If you say so, but that twinkle in your eye is telling something very different."

"I'll admit, Desmond Blackwell is freakin' hot. Think Denzel Washington in his prime with some serious street edge in the mix."

"Get the fuck outta here! No wonder your eyes are dancing around like a six-year-old ballerina. Maybe I need to call Amir and tell him to get his ass to Miami ASAP before his girl get stole."

"Don't you dare!" Justina giggled. "Like I said, we're cool nothing more than that."

That's what Justina's mouth was saying, but the tingle between her legs was singing a different tune.

Taren slid a paper plate full of bullshit food over to Dominique. She was starving, so the cut up hot dogs and baked beans tasted like filet mignon and lobster. She was stuffing the food down her throat like it was her last meal. That didn't stop Taren from holding her gun steady to the side of Dominique's head in case she got any bright ideas. She washed everything down with bottled water.

"Can I have some more?" Dominique begged while chewing the last piece of meat.

"Hell no! You better be lucky I gave you that." Taren wasn't lying. For the last few days all she had been giving her prisoner were loafs of bread and Kool-Aid. The only reason she gave Dominique the beans and franks was because it was leftovers she didn't want.

"You've kept me alive for over a week now does that mean eventually you're going to let me go?" Dominique mumbled. She didn't expect a positive response, but she was just trying to delay being put back in the dark closet. At least being out in the living room there were lights, and visuals coming from the television.

"What do you think?" Taren smacked.

"I don't know what to think anymore."

"Let me ask you a question, is there a back way to get inside the strip club you work at?"

"Yes, but we don't use it."

"Then who uses it?"

"Mostly the kitchen staff and the people who take the trash out."

"Does security use that back door?"

"No, not that I've ever seen. It's connected to an alley so it's pretty dark. Most people don't like to use that door."

"That's good to know."

"Are you planning on leaving me there?" Dominique questioned with optimism in her voice. "If you did, nobody would probably even notice. You could be in and out without being detected. Like I told you, I wouldn't tell anyone what happened."

Taren had to stop herself from bursting out laughing. She found what Dominique said to be hysterical, but she thought it was best to keep her prisoner in the dark. "As a matter of fact that's exactly what I'm planning on doing," she said, which wasn't a complete lie.

"Really?! When?"

"This Friday. In case you've lost track of time that's in two days," Taren informed Dominique.

"Omigosh, you're letting me go in two days. Thank you so much!" Dominique began to cry. "I promise I will not tell anybody what happened. I'll say I went back home to visit my family or that some men wearing masks kidnapped me and I have no idea who they were. Whatever you want me to say."

Taren could see the fear and desperation in Dominique's eyes. She knew her victim would keep her mouth shut. If Taren wasn't planning to commit the ultimate revenge, she would really consider letting Dominique live, but it wasn't in the cards.

"Listen, I have to run some errands so back in the closet you go. Now remember, you better be a good girl. When I come back if I see anything suspicious I'll have to kill you."

"I won't do anything especially now that I know I'll be going home soon," Dominique said with newfound assurance.

"Smart girl. I'll see you when I get back," Taren said, putting duct tape over Dominique's mouth then handcuffing her hands and feet.

Taren had a lot of shopping to do to prepare for Friday's celebration.

"You're telling me it's been over a week and you have nothing regarding Dominique's where-abouts? She didn't fuckin' vanish! Did you get in touch with her family?" Desmond wanted to know.

"I did and no one has been in touch with her. Boss, there's a good chance Dominique is dead and whoever killed her disposed of the body."

"I don't wanna hear that shit, Sammie. With Aspen dead and Dominique missing the cops are on my ass. Fuck!" Desmond scoffed knocking over some items on his desk. "I wanted this shit to be resolved before this party Friday, but it ain't gonna happen."

"No, it's not, but there's a few other people I still need to speak with. Including that guy Rico the dancer mentioned to you."

"What's the hold up?"

"He's on the road traveling. He does security work so he's constantly in and out of Miami. Honestly I doubt he'll be much help anyway."

"Why you say that?"

"I ran a check on the girl, Taren, and she's

clean. I even followed her for a couple days and nothing. She goes to the gym, work, and back home. I think whatever suspicion Aspen had was baseless. You know women can be catty sometimes."

"No doubt, but go see that dude Rico whenever he gets back in town. You need to follow every lead. I don't care how baseless it might seem."

"I'm on it boss."

Desmond sat down behind his desk after Sammie left. His frustration was getting the best of him. He was used to resolving problems not hitting brick walls. With the murder of Laurie and Aspen he believed that maybe someone had it out for Angel, but with Dominique possibly being dead it was throwing him off. She didn't work for Angel's Girls she worked directly for him. So now Desmond was contemplating if someone had a grudge against him. He always tried to play it straight, but in his line of business things could get murky at times. The more questions were raised the more determined he was to get answers. Desmond had also taken a special liking to Dominique. He was the one that had discovered her in that rundown strip club and brought her to Miami. He promised to give Dominique the life she always dreamed of and Desmond prided himself on being a man of his word.

Chapter Twenty-Two

A Night To Remember

"You seem to get more beautiful everyday," Darien said admiring Angel as she looked at herself in the mirror.

"I wasn't sure if this dress was too risqué, but once I put it on I think it works." Angel smiled.

"Perfection doesn't do you justice," he said gazing at Angel in the sheer black lace Givenchy couture gown. The super sultry look was complimented with strappy black Manolo Blahnik sandals. "I have the sexiest wife in the world." Darien pulled Angel in close, kissing her soft lips.

"Thank you my love. You always know the right words to say. Now let's get out of here before I slip outta this dress and rip off your tuxedo because you are looking pretty damn delectable yourself."

"I love when you flirt with me," Darien said taking his wife's hand.

When Angel and Darien arrived at Diamonds & Pearls the red carpet event was in full effect. The street was lined up with nothing but Ferraris, Lambos, Maybachs, and Bugattis. It looked like an elite car show for the rich and famous.

"It appears your partner went all out," Darien commented as they stepped out the car.

"Desmond doesn't like to spare any expenses. He claims the money has to look like it's always flowing to get it to actually flow." Angel laughed.

"Excuse me?"

"I know, babe. You can't put too much thought into what Desmond says. You simply nod your head in agreement and keep it moving. But there's no denying, whatever he's doing it works."

"You won't get an argument from me. I remember there was a lot of buzz surrounding this club when it first opened. I never had a chance to come through, but it's nice in here," Darien said walking through the front entrance into opulence. The first thing he noticed was the custom DJ booth and suspended performance platform, all enveloped with floor to ceiling LED screens. On the main level the VIP booths surrounded the dance floor as strippers glided up platinum and diamond studded poles. Desmond had created a plush strip club that was unlike any other.

"Hi, I'm Nicole. I'll be your waitress for the evening. Please follow me to your booth," she said to Angel and Darien. She escorted them to a center booth right next to Aaliyah and Dale.

"Baby, come with me. I want you to meet my sister." Darien had never seen Angel so giddy. She saw Aaliyah's eyes widen when she got near. Angel wasn't sure if it was a look of joy, surprise or I don't want to be bothered with you.

"Angel, you look amazing," Aaliyah said giving her a hug.

"So do you! I wanted you to meet my husband. Darien this is my sister Aaliyah."

"Pleasure. My wife has spoken very highly of you so it's good to finally meet you," Darien said shaking Aaliyah's hand.

"You don't have to be so formal. We're family. Give me a hug. I want you all to meet my fiancé," Aaliyah said, waving Dale to come over. "Baby, this is Angel and her husband..."

"Darien Blaze! What's good! I'm a huge fan of yours," Dale said shaking Darien's hand. "Angel, it's great to finally meet you. Aaliyah, why didn't you tell me your sister was married to the champ?!" Dale questioned glancing at her with confusion.

"I could've sworn I did. Well, now you know." Aaliyah giggled nervously. "Justina, come here so you can meet Angel," Aaliyah said wanting to switch it up since she was mad that Dale called her out about Darien.

"So you're Angel. Wow, stunning indeed," Justina remarked then placing her attention on Darien. "And you're Darien Blaze. Are you all here together?"

"Yes, Darien is my husband." Angel smiled sweetly.

"Oh wow! You look like this and you're married to the welterweight champion of the world. I get it." Justina nodded. Angel stared at her oddly before Aaliyah grabbed her arm.

"Excuse me, I need to talk to my best friend for a minute." Aaliyah grinned, pulling Justina away. "Did you have to be anymore obvious," Aaliyah hissed.

Justina laughed hysterically before covering her mouth. "I'm sorry! But this is hilarious."

"What is so funny?"

"You're sister. Could her life be anymore enviable? You never said she was that hot and her husband was equally hot and freakin' loaded."

"Maybe I forgot to mention she was married to Darien Blaze, but I did tell you she was gorgeous."

"Gorgeous and hot are two totally different things. A girl can be gorgeous and not hot whatsoever. But listen you're equally as gorgeous and equally as hot. I'm just saying I get it now. You're used to being the star and now you have to share that spotlight. I mean gosh, did you see her in that dress?" Justina glanced back over at Angel who was talking to her husband and Dale. "I think that might be Givenchy too, but hell her husband's loaded, so I'm sure she can afford couture. Your fiancé is clearly also a fan of Darien's."

Aaliyah scowled up her face ready to smack the shit out of Justina. This was her night and her party. She didn't need her best friend salivating over her newly found sister. "Enough about Angel. I need a drink and some fresh air. Come with me," Aaliyah said.

"Sure, let me grab my purse off the table." Justina used this opportunity to send a text to Nesa. The stage had been set all Nesa had to do was deliver the dialogue. "Got it! Let's go get that drink and step outside.

Aaliyah was making Justina's plan go even smoother than she thought it would. She figured her biggest obstacle was going to be putting enough space and time between Aaliyah and Dale to allow Nesa to do her thing. But with Angel showing up and Justina going overboard with the compliments, it put Aaliyah in such a foul mood she had no interest in being around anyone including her future husband.

Angel sat down in the booth and had a glass of champagne while Darien and Dale kicked it like they had known each other all their lives. She noticed Aaliyah and Justina walk out and was tempted to follow behind, but then she got a text from Taren.

Hey! I'm on the way. Just checking to see if you got to the party yet. If you have save me a dance ☺

***Yep! Already here and so are the other
girls. Hurry up the party is fab!***

Angel decided she would wait until Taren
arrived before tracking down Aaliyah so she
could introduce them. She was excited for Taren
to meet her sister and hoped the three of them
would be close. "I'm surprised to see you back
so soon," Angel said when Darien sat down next
to her. "You and Dale were over there talking like
you were the best of friends."

"He's a cool guy. I like him. The only reason I
left was because that dancer came over. She said
something about Desmond wanting her to give
him a dance."

"I see. Not sure if Aaliyah would approve,"
Angel said looking over at Dale and the scantily
clad woman.

"This is a strip club and it's a party. A dance
from a stripper is harmless."

"I know that and you know that, but something tells me Aaliyah wouldn't go for it. I could
be wrong." Angel shrugged.

"Luckily, Aaliyah stepped away. By the time
she comes back, I'm sure the dancer will be gone
and all is good," Darien said, clapping his hands.

"I'm sure you're right." For a second when
Angel glanced back over at Dale they locked eyes

before his attention returned to the stripper. He seemed to be listening intently to something she was saying and Angel couldn't help but wonder what that was.

"Yo hold up!" Dale grabbed on Nesa's arm roughly, but she kept her cool. She already knew he would be rattled by what she said and Nesa was a pro at dealing with disgruntled customers. "What the fuck did you just say to me?" Dale needed to hear the shit again.

"I knew your brother Emory. I was cool with him and this other nigga he dealt with named Arnez. I spoke to Arnez right after your brother got killed. He told me he knew who murdered Emory and was going to get retribution because he had mad love for him."

"You're telling me that this nigga Arnez told you he knew who killed my brother?"

"Yes. But I lost contact with Arnez. I don't know what happened to him. So when I saw you, I thought maybe you would know. I mean I assumed you were cool with Arnez too."

Nesa could see Dale's anger begin to simmer and what she would tell him next would bring it to the boiling point. "So who did Arnez say killed my brother?"

"That's the thing; I didn't' believe Arnez had

the right guy. That maybe he was mistaken."

"Why did you think that?"

"Because he said it was Supreme. You know that guy that used to be a big-time rapper. I mean why would a man like Supreme want to kill Emory. That didn't make any sense to me. Does that make any sense to you?" By the time Nesa asked that question Dale had bolted and she had a pretty good idea exactly where he was headed.

It's time to go," Taren said to Dominique as she grabbed her bag and they headed to a rental car she had gotten.

"I hope you don't mind me asking but is there a reason you're dressed like that?" Dominique asked observing Taren's long dark wig which hid her cropped blonde hair, a baseball cap, and a dark sweatsuit although it was damn near one hundred degrees outside.

"Just taking precaution. I know you said no one really uses that back door and I won't be seen, but you can never be too careful. That's also why I'm keeping you handcuffed on our ride to the club."

"That makes sense."

"Although I'm being careful I'm still counting on you to keep your word," Taren said wanting Dominique to believe nothing bad was going to happen to her.

"Of course... you have my word. Nobody will ever know about you or what happened."

"That's my girl. I'ma need you to tell me the best way for us to get to that exit door without being seen."

"No problem. There's a back street that leads into the alley where the door is. A lot of delivery trucks pull in that way," Dominique informed her captor wanting to be as helpful as possible believing freedom was within her reach.

As they got closer to the club, Dominique began directing Taren how to go without being seen. After they parked, Taren kept the handcuffs on Dominique's hands, but took off the ones on her ankles so she could walk. The way they went was extremely dark as there were no streetlights.

"That's the door right there," Dominique lifted her arms the best that she could to show Taren.

"Let's wait a few minutes to make sure no one is coming in or out. Also, don't be alarmed, but I have to put this blindfold over your eyes. It's for your protection too. You know for your story to sound believable," Taren said convincingly.

"Got you."

"Remember the kidnapping story we discussed. Make sure you stick to it because the cops are going to grill you."

"I've remembered every word," Dominique assured her not having a clue that it didn't even matter.

"Okay, it's show time. Let's go."

Taren and Dominique rushed to the door, which was slightly ajar just like Dominique said it would be. Taren opened it and could hear the loud music blaring from the speakers, but there was no one in the hallway right by the door. As Dominique stood in the doorway, Taren took the gun out of her book bag and pounded it over Dominique's head knocking her out cold. Taren quickly dragged her body inside and left it in the corner slightly hidden away. Taren stood in the same corner and took out the star of the show. The homemade bomb she meticulously put together.

Taren came up with the bomb idea after watching a show on Investigation Discovery. She had no idea that a simple Google search would give her a step-by-step blueprint on how to build the perfect bomb. In a few short minutes Taren felt confident she would get rid of everyone that she considered a problem. It didn't even bother her that hundreds of innocent people who had absolutely nothing to do with her vendetta against Angel would die in the process. If she had to take out an entire nightclub to get to the one person she considered an enemy then so be it.

Once Taren placed the bomb in a prime location she exited out the same door she came in without detection. She waited until she was safely back in her rental car and was driving off before detonating the bomb. All Taren saw was a massive explosion in her rearview mirror as she drove off into the night.

Coming soon!!

All I See Is The Money…

Female Hustler 4

A Novel

JOY DEJA KING

SUPREME

JOY DEJA KING

Chapter One

I Will Be King

From my very first recollection as a kid, I remember staring my parents directly in their eyes while sitting at the dinner table and stating without hesitation, "I will be king." I then looked back down at my plate of food and continued to eat.

"Xavier, what did you say?" my mother questioned, seeming completely bewildered by my comment.

"I said, I'll be king," I repeated, shrugging my shoulders in a nonchalant way. Even then at the age of four or five I had this I don't give a fuck aura about myself. When I was younger, people mistook it as me being disengaged from others. When I got older, people labeled me as arrogant, but honestly it was none of the above. I just knew, I always knew, that I would be somebody great, that I would leave a legacy that my children and grandchildren would admire and respect.

"Boy, what are you talking about now?" My dad chuckled, glancing over at my mother. "You always talking crazy. I tell you what you gon' be… a damn comedian." He laughed. My dad didn't mean any harm, he just didn't know any better.

I didn't even respond to my dad. Once again I shrugged my shoulders and continued eating my dinner. At that time, I wasn't sure the path in life I would take that would make me king. I was only sure that greatness awaited me and I was looking forward to taking my spot on the throne.

"Only one more week of school and then summer vacation… yes!" I shouted, pumping my fist in the air.

"It ain't gonna be no vacation for me. I have to go to summer school," my friend, Isaac, complained as we walked home from school.

"I still don't understand how you flunking classes in the 8th grade. I mean we don't even do shit," I said, shaking my head.

"Whatever, Xavier. Everybody can't be a fuckin' genius like you. You don't even have to open a book and already know all the answers. You've always been that way," Isaac huffed, shaking his head.

"You got excuses for everything." I shrugged, quickly losing interest in the conversation because my thirteen-year-old eyes were fixated on the lyrical battle taking place right in front of me. There was a small crowd surrounding the guys who looked to be only a few years older than me. As I walked closer, not only was I able to witness but I could hear them spitting lyrics back and forth to each other. It was a word battle that I had never seen before and the more the verbiage escalated the more intrigued I became.

"Xavier, come on! We need to get home," I heard Isaac call out, but I was paying him no mind. I wanted in on the battle. It was crazy. I had never rapped a lyric a day in my life, but hearing these two young guys who looked just like me, going at it had me mesmerized. Yeah, I had watched rappers on television and heard them on the radio, but being so up close and personal had this profound affect on me.

"Yo, Xavier we need to go!" Isaac yelled, grabbing my arm. "You know I'm on punishment. My moms told me I betta come straight home after school. So let's go or I'ma get in trouble," Isaac complained.

"Man, stop yo' whining. Besides, you on punishment… not me. Take yo' ass home. I'ma stay here and watch this rap battle," I said dropping my book bag. I was ready to make this corner block my home for the rest of the afternoon.

"Yo' you buggin'! I thought you were gon' come to my house and keep me company. My mom said you the only friend I can have over."

"Go 'head." I waved my hand, signaling Isaac to keep it moving. "I'll be over there in a minute."

Isaac glanced at me and then the two guys rapping. "Why you so interested in what they doing?" he questioned, not able to hide his confusion. It was written all over his face.

"'Cause they doing what I'ma do." I nodded my head with confidence.

"And what's that… run yo' mouth? You already know how to do that."

"Nah, dummy!" I shook my head. "I'ma be a rapper."

Isaac fell out laughing. He bent over, dropping his book bag, making this major production like he heard the funniest joke ever. "X, you got mad jokes. So you gon' be on the corner like these two clowns and call yo'self a rapper," he sneered. Isaac was now holding his stomach like he was laughing so hard that he had stomach cramps or something.

"Go 'head… keep laughing." I chuckled. "Wait and see. Not only am I gonna be a rapper. But the streets gon' say I was wanna the best that ever did it. I'ma be a star." Then I paused for a second before continuing. "Fuck a star. I'ma be a superstar." I smiled looking towards the clouds, seeing my vision up in the blue sky."

"Yo, you have officially lost yo' mind," Isaac snorted. "When you get yo' head up outta those clouds, stop by the crib. I'll be waiting on you so we can play some video games."

"Cool." I nodded as Isaac hurried off, but I never made it to his crib that day. I stayed on the block like my shoes were glued to the cement. That afternoon, on a sunny day in Queens, New York, I realized just how I would create my legacy. "Get ready world, 'cause I will be king," I mumbled under my breath as I continued to study the two young men who had become my inspiration.

The Legacy

Keep The Family Close...

Raised By Wolves

Chapter One

"Alejo, we've been doing business for many years and my intention is for there to be many more. But I do have some concerns..."

"That's why we're meeting today," Alejo interjected, cutting Allen off. I've made you a very wealthy man. You've made millions and millions of dollars from my family..."

"And you've made that and much more from our family," Clayton snapped, this time being the one to cut Alejo off. "So lets acknowledge this being a mutual beneficial relationship between both of our families."

Alejo cut his eyes at Clayton, feeling disrespected his anger rested upon him. Clayton was the youngest son of Allen Collins but also the most vocal. Alejo then turned towards his eldest son

Damacio who sat calmly not saying a word in his father's defense, which further enraged the dictator of the Hernandez family.

An ominous quietness engulfed the room as the Collins family remained seated on one side of the table and the Hernandez family occupied the other.

"I think we can agree that over the years we've created a successful business relationship that works for all parties involved," Kasir spoke up and said, trying to be the voice of reason and peacemaker for what was quickly turning into enemy territory. "No one wants to create new problems. We only want to fix the one we currently have so we can all move forward."

"Kasir, I've always liked you," Alejo said with a half smile. "You've continuously conducted yourself with class and respect. Others can learn a lot from you."

"Others, meaning your crooked ass nephews," Clayton barked not ignoring the jab Alejo was taking at him. He then pointed his finger at Felipe and Hector, making sure that everyone at the table knew exactly who he was speaking of since there was a dozen family members on the Hernandez side of the table.

Chaos quickly erupted within the Hernandez family as the members began having a heated exchange amongst each other. They were speaking Spanish and although Allen nor Clayton understood what was being said, Kasir spoke the language fluently.

"Dad, I think we need to fall back and not let this meeting get any further out of control. Lets table this discussion for a later date," Kasir told his father in a very low tone.

"Fuck that! We ain't tabling shit. As much money as we bring to this fuckin' table and these snakes want to short us. Nah, I ain't having it. That shit ends today," Clayton stated, not backing down.

"You come here and insult me and my family with your outrageous accusations," Alejo stood up and yelled, pushing back the single silver curl that kept falling over his forehead. I will not tolerate such insults from the likes of you. My family does good business. You clearly cannot say the same."

"This is what you call good business," Clayton shot back, placing his iPhone on the center of the table. Then pressing play on the video that was sent to him.

Alejo grabbed the phone from off the table and watched the video intently, scrutinizing every detail. After he was satisfied he then handed it to his son Damacio, who after viewing, passed it around to the other family members at the table.

"What's on that video?" Kasir questioned his brother.

"I want to know the same thing," his father stated.

"Lets just say that not only is those two motherfuckers stealing from us, they stealing from they own fuckin' family too," Clayton huffed, leaning back in his chair, pleased that he had the proof to back up his claims.

"We owe your family an apology," Damacio said, as his father sat back down in his chair with a glaze of defeat in his eyes. It was obvious the old man hated to be wrong and had no intentions of admitting it, so his son had to do it for him.

"Does that mean my concerns will be addressed and handled properly?" Allen Collins questioned.

"Of course. You have my word that this matter will be corrected in the very near future and there is no need for you to worry, as it won't happen again. Please accept my apology on behalf of my entire family," Damacio said, reaching over to shake each of their hand.

"Thank you, Damacio," Allen said giving a firm handshake. "I'll be in touch soon."

"Of course. Business will resume as usual and we look forward to it," Damacio made clear before the men gathered their belongings and began to make their exit.

"Wait!" the Collins men stopped in their tracks and turned towards Alejo who had shouted for them to wait.

"Father, what are you doing?" Damacio asked, confused by his father's sudden outburst.

"There is something that needs to be addressed and no one is leaving this room until it's done," Alejo demanded.

With smooth ease, Clayton rested his arm towards the back of his pants, placing his hand on the Glock 20-10mm auto. Before the meeting, the Collins' men had agreed to have their security team wait outside in the parking lot instead of coming in the building, so it wouldn't be a hostile environment. But that didn't stop Clayton from taking his own precautions. He eyed his brother Kasir who maintained his typical calm demeanor that annoyed the fuck out of Clayton.

"Alejo, what else needs to be said that wasn't already discussed?" Allen asked, showing no signs of distress.

"Please, come take a seat," Alejo said politely. Allen stared at Alejo then turned to his two sons and nodded his head as the three men walk back towards their chairs.

Alejo wasted no time and immediately began his over the top speech. "I was born in Mexico and raised by wolves. I was taught that you kill or be killed. When I rose to power by slaughtering my enemies and my friends, I felt no shame." Alejo stated looking around at everyone sitting at the table. His son Damacio swallowed hard as his adam's apple seemed to be throbbing out of his neck.

"As I got older and had my own family, I decided I didn't want that for my children. I wanted them to understand the importance of loyalty, honor and respect," Alejo said proudly, speaking with his thick Spanish accent, which was heavier than usual. He moved away from his chair and began to pace the floor as his spoke. "Without understanding the meaning of being loyal, honoring and respecting your family, you're worthless. Family forgives but some things are unforgivable so you have no place on this earth or in my family."

Then without warning and before anyone had even noticed, all you saw was blood squirting from Felipe's slit throat. Then with the same precision and quickness, Alejo took his sharp pocketknife and slit Hector's throat too. Everyone was too stunned and taken aback to stutter a word.

Alejo then wiped the blood off his pocketknife on the white shirt that a now dead Felipe was wearing. He kept wiping until the knife was clean. "That is what happens when you are disloyal. It will not be tolerated...ever." Alejo made direct contact with each of his family member at the round table then focused on Allen. "I want to personally apologize to you and your sons. I do not condone what Felipe and Hector did and they have now paid the price with their lives."

"Apology accepted," Allen said.

"Yeah, now lets get the fuck outta here," Clayton whispered to his father as the three men stood in unison not speaking another word until they were out the building.

"What type of shit was that?" Kasir mumbled.

"I told you that old man was fuckin' crazy," Clayton said shaking his head as they got into their waiting SUV.

"I think we all knew he was crazy just not that crazy. Alejo know he could've slit them boys throats after we left," Allen huffed. "He just wanted us to see the fuckin' blood too and ruin our after-noon," he added before chuckling.

"I think it was more than just that," Clayton re-plied, looking out the tinted window as the driver pulled out the parking lot.

"Then what?" Kasir questioned.

"I think old man Alejo was trying to make a point, not only to his family members but to us too."

"You might be right, Clayton."

"I know I'm right. We need to keep all eyes on Alejo 'cause I don't trust him. He might've killed his crooked ass nephews to show good faith but trust me that man hates to ever be wrong about anything. What he did to those nephews is proba-bly what he really wanted to do to us but he knew nobody would've left that building alive. The only truth Alejo spoke in there was that he was raised by wolves," Clayton scoffed leaning back in the car seat.

All three men remained silent for the dura-tion of the drive. Each pondering what had trans-pired in what was supposed to be a simple busi-ness meeting that turned into a double homicide. They also thought about the point Clayton said

Alejo was trying to make. No one wanted that to be true as their business with the Alejo family was a lucrative one for everyone involved. But for men like Alejo, sometimes pride held more value than the almighty dollar, which made him extremely dangerous.

Bitch

Bitch Reloaded

Bitch Is Back

Queen Bitch

Last Bitch Standing

Bitch A New Beginning

Boss Bitch

Bad Bitch

Still The Baddest Bitch

Read
The Entire
Bitch Series in
This Order

Bitch The Begginning Of The End

A KING PRODUCTION

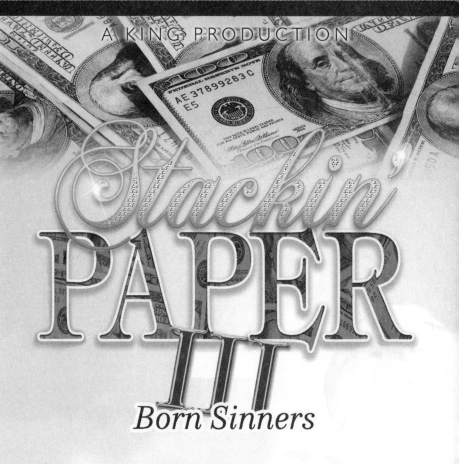

Stackin' PAPER III

Born Sinners

a novel

JOY DEJA KING